Henrietta Christian Wright

Children's Stories in English Literature

From Taliesin to Shakespeare

Henrietta Christian Wright

Children's Stories in English Literature
From Taliesin to Shakespeare

ISBN/EAN: 9783337071615

Printed in Europe, USA, Canada, Australia, Japan

Cover: Foto ©Andreas Hilbeck / pixelio.de

More available books at **www.hansebooks.com**

CHAPTER XIII.

CHAPTER XIV.

CHAPTER XV.

CHAPTER I.

Once upon a time a company of daring seamen from the eastern borders of the North Sea,
sailing the ocean in search of new adventures,
came to a land whose white cliffs had seemed
to shine a welcome to them for many a mile
across the gray waters. This was the country
now known as England, but then called Britain;
and the seamen found it to be a green and
pleasant land, with safe coasts and good har-
bors, and inhabited by a race like themselves,
brave, strong, and warlike, always eager for
battle, and happiest when engaged in deadly
combat with some foe as fierce and unrelenting
as themselves.

The new-comers stayed long enough to
learn something of the life and customs of the
strangers—and perhaps had a battle or two

with them in order to try their mettle—and then sailed away again; and when they returned home told their friends wonderful stories of the Britons—those island warriors—and their brave deeds; of their terrible appearance in battle, with their dark hair floating back from their foreheads, and the upper part of their bodies naked and covered with pictures of monsters and demons, and of their savage warcries, and their war-chariots with their wheels furnished with sharp scythes to cut down the opposing foemen.

And they told also of the wide-stretching meadows, and fine rivers, and great forests filled with all kinds of game; and of their walled cities and beautiful temples, which had been built by Roman conquerors when they claimed the island for their own.

These stories spread from one tribe to another until all the people living on the eastern borders of the North Sea knew about the Land of the Sea-Cliffs; and many voyages were made thither. We do not exactly know the date when these foreign tribes first began to visit Britain, though it was probably about the year 350; but from that time it was no uncommon thing for the Britons to see these strangers landing on their coasts. And as time passed the visitors, who had first been attracted by curiosity, or love of gain, or friendship—for the Britons more than once asked their help in the wars that they had with unfriendly tribes in the north—came gradually to consider the country as their own, and built homes there in the shades of the deep forests, or on the borders of the sea, and the ancient inhabitants were regarded by them almost as intruders.

Then for two hundred years or more there were wars over all the country, and as the strangers were more and more successful, and made settlement after settlement, even the old name Britain began to be seldom heard, and the country was called the land of the Angles, or Saxons, or Jutes, after the different tribes of invaders.

The Britons who were thus made to fight for their homes were a race hard to conquer. Even the Roman soldiers, who subdued almost

all of Europe, never really conquered these isl-
and warriors, and only succeeded in living har-
moniously with them when they offered them
friendship and taught them the arts of peace,
instead of trying to make slaves of them.

Their religion was a gloomy and forbidding
one, but taught them to die like heroes, and to
fear nothing except the anger of their priests,
who were called Druids, and who held unlim-
ited power over the people. They worshipped
sometimes in the great stone temples, round
and roofless, which were built in the open plain,
and sometimes in the groves that were consecrated to religious uses. And as the solemn
ceremony proceeded, and the prisoners taken
in battle were brought forward and sacrificed
upon the altars, the warriors felt that they too
were connected with the mysterious rites that
held such awe for them, and believed all the
more firmly that war was a glorious thing, and
to die in battle the only death for a brave man.

The treasures taken in battle were kept in
the sacred groves, unguarded; for so great was
the fear of the Druids and their power that not

even the bravest chieftain would approach the spot; and this custom gave them an added terror as foemen, for no prize of gold or silver or jewel offered by the enemy as the price of peace could compare in value, to the British warrior, with the branch of oak or twig of mistletoe which the priests bestowed upon him as the reward of valor.

Thus loving war and content with their rough mode of life, nothing that an enemy could offer would seem worth accepting; and although the Romans built walled cities, and laid out gardens and vineyards, and reclaimed the forest lands from the wild beasts, the nature of the people did not change very much. And thus, notwithstanding the centuries of Roman influence which preceded, the sea-kings who came to conquer Britain for their own found its people as savage and war-loving as themselves, and the conflict between them was a bitter one.

It was natural that as war was the thing that engaged the thoughts of the people most, it should also form the subject of their songs, and the sweetest singer, in the mind of the British chieftain, was he who could best praise the warlike deeds of his chief, and predict honor and glory for him in the future. From the earliest times it was the custom among them for each chieftain or king to have certain bards and singers attached to his court, whose duty it was to recount his deeds of battle and those of his forefathers, to relate the history of ancient times, to sing the glories of the present, and to prophesy future victories. These minstrels held places of high importance, and took rank with the chief officers of the household.

Sometimes, when war had ceased for awhile, the warriors would resume their old pastimes, and hunt the wolves, bears, deer, and boars that roamed almost unchecked through the vast forests; and after the hunt, as they lay around the great fires weary with the day's slaughter, the bards would sing other songs more peaceful in character, and partaking somewhat of the nature of their rough, but cherished home-life. And from the fragments of these songs that have come down to us, we are able to judge somewhat of the manner of living in those far-off times.

One of these old British lays relates the story of Crede, a beautiful princess of Kerry, who declared she would marry no one but a poet capable of describing her house. And then we see the picture of the young poet stepping out into the midst of the gay company, wearing a crimson cloak fastened with a gold brooch, and bearing his gold-rimmed shield, and gold-hilted sword, and shining spear, which he stands against the side of the hall while he takes the harp and sings of the beauty of Crede's house. And from his song we learn that the house of the beautiful princess was well worthy of her. It was a hundred spans from one corner to another, and the heavy oaken door was twenty feet wide, with a lintel of carved silver, and posts of green bronze, and a portico thatched with wings of blue and yellow birds. Inside, the corner-stones were of silver and gold, and the floor was covered with green rushes. There were beautiful couches from the East, adorned with yellow gold and precious stones, and with embroidered curtains hanging from bronze rods; and there were chairs blazing with jewels, and silken gowns and blue mantles, and red and gold and crystal cups; and there was the great bronze vat filled with the " pleasant juice of the malt," and the cup-bearers clad in rich raiment passing to and fro among the guests bearing jewelled goblets filled with mead, and serving cakes and fruits; and there were songs and laughter and merry words, for Crede's house was always filled with guests, all of whom received cordial welcome, from the wandering musicians who paid for their welcome with a song, to the stern and solemn Druids who awed the children with their grave silence.

Such was the Song of Crede—sung by the brave young harper who was suing for her love, and listened to with critical attention by the gathered company who desired that the praises of their fair princess and her beautiful house should be celebrated in words and music the most fitting.

And then there was the song of Bailé, the Sweet-spoken, and the Princess Aillin, which tells how the unfortunate pair, being crossed in love and parted by bitter fate, set out to meet each other privately on the banks of the Boyne; and how, as Bailé and his followers were resting, having unyoked their chariots and sent their horses out to graze, they saw a horrible spectre like a man coming toward them along the shore, "swiftly as the hawk darts from the cliff or the wind rushes from off the sea." And he told Bailé that Aillin was dead, as had been foretold by the Druids, and that they would never meet in life, but would meet after death and would not part forever after that. And then the man passed by "as a blast of the wind," and Bailé fell dead of the evil tidings, and his tombstone was set up, and a yew grew up through his grave and the form of Bailé's head appeared on the top of it. And then the horrible spectre sped southward, and passed into the sunny chamber of Aillin, and told her he had witnessed the lamentations over Bailé who died while coming to meet her. Then Aillin fell dead, and her tombstone was set up and an apple-tree grew through her grave and became a great tree, and Aillin's head appeared on the top of it. And at the end of seven years the two trees were cut down by the poets and prophets and seers, and were made into two tablets, on which were written the loves of Bailé and Aillin. And long afterward, at a great festival of the bards of the realm, the poets came from the North bringing the tablet of yew, and the poets came from the South bringing the tablet of applewood, and as the lord of the festival held the two tablets in his hands, in order to read the tragic story engraven thereon, suddenly they sprang together and were united so firmly that they could not possibly be separated. And they were preserved many years in the treasury at Tara, until it was burned by an enemy of the land.

Among the most popular of these old songs were those of Taliesin, one of the greatest of the old bards. Taliesin, whose name meant Shining Forehead, and was given him on ac-

count of the wondrous beauty of his counte-
nance, was one of those fascinating personages
whom the early races delighted to surround
with mystery. There were strange accounts
of his birth, some asserting that he was the son
of an enchanter and knew all the secrets of the
past and the mysteries of the future, as well as
the voices of nature in the world around, and
that he had come from his home in the region
of the summer stars to encourage man by his
songs and prophecies.

Many of the songs relate to the victories of
the great British chief Urien, which took place
between the years 547 and 560. Taliesin is
supposed to have passed many years of his
life at the court of Urien, where he was chief
bard, and at all the great feasts the warriors
listened in astonishment and delight while Taliesin sang in a voice of unrivalled sweetness
and power the deeds of their famous chieftain.
He boasted always of Urien's exploits with
loyal enthusiasm, Urien, whose rage was a
sword and whose spirit inspired his followers,
charging them to keep their faces ever toward

the foe and raise their spears high above the heads of the Saxons. " Urien," he says, " is warlike, with the grandeur of a perfect prince." Urien is " the eagle of the land—he terrifies the trembling Saxon, whose destiny is a bier." And then, as the listeners bend forward more eagerly, the music swells, and the words grow more vehement. " What noise is that? Is it the earth that quakes, or the white swell of the sea rolling landward ? If there is a cry on the hill, is it not Urien that terrifies ? If there is a cry in the valley, is it not Urien thrusting his spear ? If there is a cry in the mountains, is it not Urien conquering his enemies ? If there is a sigh on the dyke, or a cry over the plains, or in the vale, it is Urien, whose spear is like death ! "

Always of Urien the bard sings lovingly and boastingly, till the great chieftain meets his death and leaves his kingdom to his sons, whom Taliesin also serves till, one by one, they fall in battle. And then Taliesin withdraws from the world and spends the rest of his life in solitary retreat in Wales, mourning the past, and sighing over the years that have left him alone and homeless.

Among the finest of his songs which do not celebrate battle, is the " Song to the Wind," one of the best examples of the old British poetry. In this poem Taliesin sings of the wind, which will never be older or younger, which is unconfined and unequalled, coming from the four regions of the earth, and flaunting his banners over every land ; unseen and seeing not, afar off and near by, bold and vehement, mute and loud-voiced, older than the earth, on sea and on land, coming unwelcome and refusing to come when desired, refusing to repair his wrong-doing and yet sinless, bearing heat of the sun and cold of the moon, without wants, and indispensable to man.

There are also a " Song to the Great World" and a " Song to the Little World," a " Song to Mead," and a " Song of Pleasant Things "—in all of which Taliesin shows that familiarity with nature and the acute perception of her beauties which are the gifts of the true poet.   The wheat on the stalk waving in the wind, the berries which the reapers gather from the hedgerows in harvest time, the sea-gulls circling on the shore, the open fields where sing the cuckoo and nightingale, the slow, long days of summer, the charlock in the springing corn, the green heath, and the salt marsh, fire, water, mist, flowers, and south winds, are all noticed with a faithful touch by this old poet, to whom nature spoke so truly and lovingly, and who knew her heart so well, that even now, after so many years, the later poet can find no meaning fairer than that given by Taliesin to the mysteries that it is the poet's gift to divine.

The later deeds of Urien were also sung by Llywarch Hen, now generally considered the greatest genius perhaps of all the old bards, though to Taliesin is given the praise of possessing the sweetest voice. Llywarch Hen was a warrior as well as bard, and followed his chief to many a bloody battle. His "Lament for Urien" is full of power and pathos, and became so popular that it was sung hundreds of years afterward by the people of the country, when chief and poet were alike almost forgotten. The minstrel-warrior was with Urien as brother-in-arms at his last great battle with the Saxons, and carried the head of his chief in his mantle from the field. The old chant is full of the horrors of that fatal day—and Llywarch sings his song with a heart full of sorrow:

> " The eagle of Gol, bold and generous,
>   Wrathful in war, sure of conquest
>   Was Urien with the ardent grasp.
>
>   A head I bear by my side,
>   The head of Urien, the leader,
>   And on his white bosom the black raven is perched ;
>
>   A head I bear in my hand,
>   He that was a soaring eagle,
>   That was the shield of his country,
>   That was a wheel in battle,
>   That was a ready sword—
>
>   A head I bear that supported me.
>   Is there any known but he welcomed ?
>   Woe to my hand, he is gone,
>   Woe to Reged from this day."

After the death of Urien, Llywarch Hen took refuge with Cyndyllan, another chief, who also fell in battle with the Saxons, who burned his house and massacred his family, and Llywarch Hen was again called upon to chant a funeral song. He sang mournfully:

"The house of Cyndyllan is gloomy this night, without fire and without song. Roofless and dark it stands, an open waste, that was once the resort of strong warriors. Without, the eagle screams loud, he has swallowed fresh drink, heart blood of Cyndyllan the fair. The house of Cyndyllan is the seat of chill grief, encircled with wide-spreading silence. Lonely it stands on the top of the rock of Hydwyth, without its lord, without guests, without the circling feasts!"

Twenty-four brave sons had Llywarch Hen, and all of them fell in fighting against their enemies. Gwenn, his best beloved, strong and large of stature, was the first to fall under the spears of the foemen, and the father's heart is filled with bitter grief as he laments for his favorite child:

"Let the wave break noisily; let it cover the shore as the lances meet in battle, let it cover the plain as the lances join in shock, for Gwenn has been slain at the ford of Morlas. O Gwenn, woe to him who is too old since he has lost you. Woe to him who is too old to avenge you! Behold the tomb of Gwenn, the fearless! Sweetly a bird sang above the head of Gwenn before they covered him with turf. But the song broke the heart of Llywarch Hen."

Llywarch Hen was also a close observer of nature, and in his descriptive poetry there is that same out-of-door freshness which distinguishes the work of Taliesin, and which is to be found in the writings of all the great English poets. In his songs of winter nothing seems to have been too small or insignificant to pass over, and every object is touched upon with the skill of the true poet; so that in reading the verses we see, as in a picture, the wet furrows, the yellow birch-tops, the bent branches bowing in the wind, the scurrying leaves, the heaps of hard grain safely housed, and hear without the war of the " gale and storm keeping equal pace."

Another time he speaks of the green-topped

birch-saplings, and the long stems of bramble, full of berries, of the thrush in her leafy nest, and the ferns drenched with showers, and the ocean veiled with the rain; he sees also the willow tops, the clover, the dog-rose, the apple blooms, the cresses and water-lilies, the hawthorn and meadow-sweet, and hears the cuckoo sing on "the blossom-covered branches, and in the ivied trees." And at night he shows us the humid glens shining under the moon, and the white-topped cliffs, and the wet beach surf-beaten and glistening, and we hear the "wave of sullen din and loud," breaking and washing over the pebbles and gravel of the shore.

Such were the songs that the old Britons listened to as they sat in the halls of their chiefs, or gathered around the blazing fires in the heart of the forest—songs of their kings and princes, and of the bloody battles fought with the enemy who had come to conquer their loved land, and of the familiar world of nature around them. It is impossible to tell positively just when these old songs were composed, for

in those early times the poetry and history of
the race were both handed down from generation to generation by word of mouth mainly.
Taliesin and Llywarch Hen, it is pretty certain,
lived in the sixth century, but, from the manner
of transmitting the old songs by word of mouth,
it might happen that a song in praise of one
chieftain would, in the next generation, be applied to another, and thus it is hard to fix a
date even for those songs which contain names
somewhat familiar to history.   But this does
not make the songs themselves any the less interesting, as for many centuries the customs
and habits of the Britons remained unchanged;
and the lays that are ascribed to Taliesin, Llywarch Hen, Anewin, Ossian, and other bards
will always have a charm for lovers of true poetry as well as for those who delight to trace the
beginnings of a nation's history.

CHAPTER II.

THE OLD SAXON SONGS.

The invaders, the fair-haired races from across the sea, who had come to drive the Britons from their homes, had also their songs, fierce and warlike as best pleased their savage natures, and well fitted to kindle in their hearts that wild enthusiasm that made them such terrible enemies in battle. Never could the harpers sing a song too fierce for these war-loving Saxons, who believed that only those who died in battle might find entrance to the hall of Odin, their chief god, and the feasts of the heroes in Valhalla.

Best liked of all these songs was that of Beowulf, the hero whose brave deeds were known to all the races living on the borders of the North Sea.   And this is the story:

Hrothgar, King of the Danes, determined to build a palace that should be forever renowned for its magnificence. So he sent all over the world for the most skilled workmen, and they came from the North and the East and the South, and in time the palace arose, stately and beautiful, and was named Heorot, from the stags' antlers which adorned the eastern and western gables. And its great mead-hall, the largest in the world, was famed among the nations for its size and splendor. Its arched roof was adorned with beautiful carvings, and its walls were hung with costly tapestry, and golden veils on which were curiously enwrought the sieges and wars of ancient times. At the upper end of the hall was the raised seat of the chief, carved in strange patterns, studded with jewels, and hung with webs of spun gold; and at the lower end stood a table which held the drinking-horns and gold and silver goblets used at the royal feasts. Through the centre of the hall, from end to end, stretched the stone hearths, on which blazed the mighty fires, and on either side of the hearths were the tables and benches for the people, the chief's " hearth-sharers." Lofty columns and pillars, carved and twined with chains of linked gold, supported the roof, and the floors were of polished wood and inlaid with rare designs. And Hrothgar was well satisfied with his beautiful palace, and ordered feasts to be held continually in the great mead-hall, where he sat in his lofty seat with his wife and nobles by his side, and listened to the songs, and distributed rings and rich gifts to all who were worthy of honor.

But evil days fell upon Heorot. One night, after a great feast, the mead-hall was entered by Grendel, the grim dragon who dwelt in the dismal fens, and was at enmity with all the races of men. The hall was full of sleeping warriors, and the hungry monster carried off thirty of Hrothgar's bravest thanes, and bore them to his den, and devoured them with greedy joy. Great was the lamentation in Heorot when the morning light disclosed the work of Grendel, and the sorrow-stricken chieftains tracked the blood-stained course of the monster to the fastnesses of the fens, and tried in vain to catch sight of their lost companions. But Grendel only mocked at their sorrow and returned to Heorot the next night, and resumed his deadly work; and despairing fear fell upon the heart of Hrothgar and his thanes, for they well knew that to war against Grendel was all in vain, for him could neither steel nor iron injure, as his scaly coat was more impenetrable than the strongest armor, and his breath was as poison to all who came near him.

Wherefore there was wailing in Hrothgar's palace night after night, for Grendel held grin sway in the mead-hall, and for twelve long years wrought sorrow in the gold-decked halls of Heorot. And the hall of feasting was deserted, and there was woe all over the land.

And the tale of distress was carried to all the neighboring kingdoms, and came to the ears of Beowulf, the Goth, bravest of Scandinavian warriors, who had in his right arm the strength of thirty men. And his heart grieved over the sorrows of Hrothgar, and he resolved if possible to free him from his enemy. So he ordered a ship to be built, and choosing fifteen of his bravest warriors, sailed away for the land of the Danes. The good ship bore them over the waters like a bird, its foam-wreathed prow glistening, and its deck filled with brave watchers; and on the second day they saw the shining cliffs and broad seanesses of Denmark.

As they sprang out on the shore they were met by the warden of the coast, who learning their errand, conducted them over the stone-paved roads until they saw the shining walls of Heorot, and then returned to the coast to guard the ship during their absence.

Beowulf and his companions entered the palace, their coats of mail glistening and their armor clanging as they traversed the long hall, and being exceedingly weary with their journey, set up their gilded shields and bucklers against the walls, piled up their long spears, and threw their war shirts in a ring on the mead benches. Then Beowulf sent Wulfgar, the king's chamberlain, to demand audience of Hrothgar, which was readily granted, for the hero's fame and nobility were well known. Then Beowulf and his warriors entered the presence of the great chief, wearing their linked war-shirts and helmets, but leaving their arms piled in the hall; and Beowulf greeted the king courteously, and also the queen and the great nobles, and said: "Hail, Hrothgar! Beowulf am I, thane and kinsman to Hygelac the Goth. Hither have I come, hearing of thy evil case, to do battle with Grendel. Oh, Prince of the bright Danes, refuse not my boon, but grant that I and my earls may fight the hero-devouring monster. Unarmed will we meet him, for he cares not for the weapons of men, and if I conquer, then will there be joy in these halls; but if I fall, send my war-shirt—wrought by the noted Weland—back to Hygelac, that he may know of my death, and that all in vain we followed the swan's path to the coasts of the Ring-Danes."

And Hrothgar answered: " Shame and sorrow have ruled long in Heorot, O Beowulf, and if thou wilt rid the land of this dreaded curse, then indeed shall praise and honor be thine from the chief of the bright Danes."

Then there was feasting and merry-making that night in the great mead-hall, and Wealtheow the queen, clad in gold-embroidered garments, bore to the guests costly jewelled goblets, and passed to and fro with her maidens distributing gifts to the heroes. And when the feast was over, one by one the Ring-Danes withdrew from the hall and left Beowulf and his companions alone ; and the Goths lay down to rest with anxious hearts, scarce expecting ever to see again their country and friends.

Then through the darkness came Grendel, creeping from the misty moors, and laughed as he entered the great mead-hall and saw the sleeping warriors. Quick as thought he seized one of the thanes, tore him limb from limb, drank his blood, and devoured him hand and foot. Then he stepped to where Beowulf lay, and seized the hero in his baleful grasp. But the Goth was awake and ready for the foe, and seized Grendel with such a grip of iron that the monster trembled with fear, for never before had he felt the strength of such a hand, and he dreaded lest his hour had come at last, and would have been glad to creep away again to the fens and leave Heorot in peace. But Beo·

wulf held him with his mighty strength, and the two joined in deadly combat. The great hall trembled under the fierce blows, and would have fallen had it not been firmly held together by its cunningly wrought bands of iron. The gold-adorned mead-benches were overturned, and the ale ran in streams over the floor. But Beowulf ceased not till he had given Grendel his death-wound, and the monster had fled to his den to die, leaving one of his hands behind him in the hall, and staining all the moors with the blood from his wounds.

Then there was joy in Heorot, and the glad news spread far and wide, and Hrothgar's thanes came riding quickly to the palace to survey the scene of the conflict. And all gazed with wonder at the wreck of the mighty hall, of which not a part was uninjured excepting the roof, and every thane felt himself honored at being permitted to see Beowulf, the hero of the fight. And then the whole company followed the track of Grendel over the noisome fens till they came to the lonely mere, and saw the surge dyed with blood and the shores shrouded with gray, poisonous vapors, and knew that the dreaded monster had crept thither to die, and that he would trouble them no more.

Then the cunning smiths set to work and forged new bands of iron, and repaired the mead-hall, which was soon made fresh by the willing hands of men and maidens, and shone at sunset as fair and beautiful as ever, hung anew with golden webs, and with its gold-adorned mead-benches waiting for the heroes. And that night the king gave a feast in honor of Beowulf, and songs were sung and mead drunk in honor of the Goth, and the king made him beautiful presents, a golden flag with jewelled standard, a helmet with the figure of the boar flashing its jewelled eyes from the crest, a coat of mail whose links were of rarest workmanship, and a sword of priceless value. And there were brought into the court eight steeds of noble size, and on one of them was a cunningly wrought saddle, blazing with gold and gems, and these also Hrothgar gave to Beowulf, and Wealtheow brought to him a cloak embroidered with gold, and a gold neck-ring of such size that it was a marvel to all be-holders, and said, "Hail, Beowulf! wear this cloak and this ring in honor of thy victory, and in token of our abiding friendship, and mayst thou be a friend to this house forever! for the praise of thy deed shall spread throughout all time, even as the waters gird all over the earth the windy walls of the land." And the feast lasted long into the night, and when it was over the warriors placed their shields, and war-shirts, and helmets, and spears at their heads and lay down to rest, fearing no evil.

But scarcely had the great hall become quiet, when, from the deadly streams that guarded the fens, came the sea-wolf, Grendel's mother, to avenge her son, and entering the hall, seized Æschere, the king's dearest thane, and bore him quickly away to her den. Now, again, there was anguish in Heorot, but again Beowulf of-fered himself as a champion, and sought the refuge of the wolf under the shadow of the hills, where black mists hung over the down-rushing streams, and a magic fire gleamed at night above the flood wherein swam dragons and serpents. And he entered the loathsome flood and sank down to the sea-wolf's dwelling, and, seizing an old sword which he saw gleaming there, forged by giants, and greater than any other man might bear, struck the murderess with the mighty brand, and slew her. The place was full of gold and gems and war weapons of strange workmanship ; but Beowulf bore away only the rich sword hilt and the head of Grendel, and so rose up again to the surface of the waters and swam to the land, and was joyfully welcomed by the warriors who had feared his death.

Then there was more rejoicing in the halls of Hrothgar, and when Beowulf finally sailed away again to his own land, his good ship could scarcely bear the weight of the treasure that Hrothgar had given him, and every man bore with him a priceless heirloom that would win him an honorable position at the court of Hygelac. And when the watchers on the coast of Norway saw the ship of Beowulf appear with its gilded boar's head flashing from the prow, they sent word in haste to the court, and the king made ready to receive the hero royally, and he was loaded with honors, and his praises were sung throughout the length and breadth of all Scandinavia.

And then the old story relates other adventures of Beowulf, and tells how he finally succeeded to the kingdom and ruled fifty years wisely, well-beloved by the people; and how he died at last, while trying to free the land from a demon who ravaged it, and so kept his bright renown to the end.

Although the story of Beowulf is, so far as its incidents are considered, a Scandinavian legend, it is, considered as literature, an English poem, and, if we except the Paraphrase of Caedmon (about which we shall hear in the next chapter, and which was written about the same time, probably), the oldest poem in the English language. It is, as a poem, not Scandinavian but English, because it is written in the language formed after the Saxons had been long in Britain and had mixed with those of the Britons whom they did not drive into Ireland,

Scotland, and Wales, and because not only the language but the scene of it is English. So far as we know, the story was never written at all before the Saxons came to Britain, and the poem is English literature in somewhat the same way (though of course by no means to the same degree) that Shakespeare's "Hamlet," for example, is English literature, though its story is taken from old Danish chronicle. All the Britons had not been driven out by the invaders, and the new race was in part British, although chiefly Anglo-Saxon, of course. And the influence of the old British songs and of the new country into which the Saxons had come, was really what gave its form and its scene to the old story retold and made into a true poem. All the scenery of the poem is English, and anyone can now find along the coast of Yorkshire the places described in it, while the country in Denmark, where the incidents of the story are supposed to have happened, is very different. It is these things as well as its early date which give the poem of Beowulf so much importance as a monument of early English literature.

The Saxons had other songs celebrating their victories over the Britons, and their adventures in the chase, and from these as well as from Beowulf we learn that, even in those early days, they held courage and brave deeds in highest honor, and valued the power of self-sacrifice. And whether we catch a glimpse of the old Britons with their tattooed bodies and floating hair rushing to battle, or wandering over the fens, or standing in solemn awe in the shadows of the deep forests where the Druids kept their treasures, guarded only by the sacredness of the place—or whether we see the conquering Saxon in his lordly hall, with his gleemen singing before him, and his earls drinking great draughts of ale, it is all a part of the same wonderful picture in which we see the England of former days, when tribe was pitted against tribe and race against race in contest for the land which each claimed so fiercely for his own.

3

CHAPTER III.

The old British songs and the story of Beowulf belong to the time before England received the name it is now known by, and when the tribes which inhabited the land were often hostile, and always jealous of the power which each held. But as years passed the land grew more peaceful, and even the old warriors who had fought so fiercely at length came to imagine a future when there should be harmony between the different tribes, and when their children's children should no longer look upon one another as rivals, but all should be joined together by mutual interests, and the word *English* stand for all the people who called that country their home.

And this time at last actually came, but in a way perhaps that the fierce sea-kings had never dreamed of, for the cause was so unlike anything that had ever influenced them, that it is no wonder they could know nothing of it. Differ as they might in many things, the Saxons and the Britons were all alike in their love for battle and the deep, undying hatred which they felt toward an invader of their homes. The British chieftain longed to die finally in battle, for his religion taught him it was the one glorious thing to do, and the Saxon chief was filled with the same desire, for the priests had taught him that only in this way could he win entrance to Valhalla, the Norseman's heaven.

But there had come to Britain from across the sea, many years before the first Saxons landed on its shores, a little band of men who neither were dressed in glittering armor, nor held in their hands the cruel weapons of war, but who wore coarse garments such as the poorest might have worn, and bore a banner on which was wrought the figure of a dove, the emblem of peace.

They were Christian missionaries who had

heard of the cruel religious practices of the Britons, and their love of revenge, and they had come to the island with the hope of winning them to a purer religion. Their simple ways of life, their honest service to their faith, their kindness to the poor, and the hope they gave of a better life beyond the grave, made a deep impression upon their listeners, who admired their courage in coming among a hostile people, sympathized with them in their indifference to hardship and deprivation, and found a strange pleasure in the thought that the new religion offered a strong field for battle, though the fighting was not to be with sword or spear, but against the strong powers of selfish courage and savage greed of power, and with the weapons of self-denial and a love that seemed all the greater because of its humility.

Many converts were won, and from this time Britain contained here and there little bands of native Christians who tried to lead their more savage brothers into gentler ways of living. Gradually churches and monasteries were established and the Christian religion was acknowledged by many, and Christian communities could be found in various places; and so extensive was the conversion that British bishops sat in the Council that was held in Arles, France, in 314, to discuss matters of importance to the Church. When the Saxon tribes came to Britain, bringing with them their religion of war and bloodshed, and finally succeeded in driving the Britons away from many places where they made Saxon settlements, the Christian religion suffered greatly from the change, and many of the British Christians went back to their ancient faith. Still, in the north of England, where the Church was too firmly established to perish before heathenism, the invaders gradually adopted the religion of the conquered, and the country became gradually re-christianized. Long afterward Christian priests from Rome came to the Saxon settlements in the south and preached the new religion of love and mercy, and in time their doctrines won favor and the southern Saxons began again to accept Christianity and to dream of another life than one of continued fighting and feasting.

Perhaps the listening warriors remembered the story of Beowulf, and how his great battle was fought with other weapons than they knew any·thing of, and how he met death gloriously while trying unselfishly to serve the people he loved ; perhaps they remembered that their great gods Odin and Thor, whose service was fear, were after all less loved by them than the gentle Baldur, whose service was peace, because all nature loved him.   At any rate, from whatever reason, the new religion gradually spread from one part of the island to another, heathen temples were pulled down, heathen gods were forsaken, and there came at last a day when England could be called a Christian land from shore to shore. And then all over the country arose monasteries and churches, and the peo-ple were more firmly united than they had ever been before, for the new faith bound one and all, high and low, in the perfect brotherhood which the monks meant to establish when they told the story of how the new faith was first preached, not to great kings or mighty war-riors, but to the humble shepherds who were watching their flocks on the hillsides around Bethlehem.

This great change could not take place without affecting the nation in many ways. War ceased to be glorified, and was looked upon as a fearful necessity and not the object of life. And the old war-songs and battle-chants gave place to Christian hymns, and it became more common to hear the sweet voices of nuns singing matins and vespers, than to start at the sound of the war-trumpet. And so it is not strange to find that about the same time that the story of Beowulf was written to please the warlike chieftains, another great poem should be sung by a Christian monk, to glorify the mission of the Church of peace, and should have for its subject the stories and incidents which are found in the Bible.

The author of this poem, known to us as Caedmon, from the name given to him by the monks when he was received into the monastery of Whitby, was born in 625, and had been perhaps, before his entrance into the community, a tenant-farmer on some of the abbey lands. In those days the lowliest born and the highest were alike in their love for song, and when we consider that their lives were for the most part spent in hard, monotonous labor, or warfare, and that what is called the beautiful had very little share in them, we do not wonder that they cherished the gift of song as the one bright thing in their existence. And so common was this gift among all classes, that it was looked upon as a reproach not to be able to sing.

According to a popular legend, Caedmon had not the gift of song at all, and felt his deficiency deeply, and this sorrow grew upon him so that he used to rise and leave the room when the harp was passed around, so that no one should see how deeply he was hurt. Thus his life was very lonely, and often sad, and as he wandered with the cattle over the meadows and heard the lark beginning the day with its sweet song, or listened to the music of the nightingale singing in the dark, when he sought to escape from the jeers of his companions, he felt that all nature had a voice and that he alone was dumb. But one night, when his friends were even merrier than usual at the feast, and the harp passed rapidly from one to another, Caedmon arose as was his custom and left the room. It was his turn to watch over the cattle during the night, and he lay down on his bed of straw and closed his eyes. But as he lay sleeping, a stranger with a face and form more beautiful than he had ever seen before, came to him in a dream, and touched him, and said, "Caedmon, sing." And Caedmon answered, "I cannot." But the stranger insisted and said, "Thou must sing." And as Caedmon looked on him he felt the birth of a new power in his soul, and his heart leaped with joy, for his visitor had brought to him the thing that he had desired above all others—the gift of song.

Then he was as eager to sing as a captive bird to use its wings, and he said to the stranger, "What shall I sing?" And he answered, "Sing me the origin of all things." Then in his dream Caedmon sang words and music that he had never heard before, in praise of the Creator of the world. And when the dream left him he still kept the music in his mind, and in the morning told the vision to an officer of the town, who led him to the Abbess Hilda, who had charge of the monastery, and who was so well beloved that everyone called her Mother. Hilda listened to Caedmon's song, and then called together all the learned men of the Order to determine the nature of his gift; for in those days it was often believed that anything uncommon might bring evil to its possessor. But as Caedmon sang, the holy men at once decided that his gift had come from heaven, for the music seemed to them divine. Then they read to Caedmon some portions of the Bible, and asked him if he could turn them into melody; and the next day he came again to the monastery and sang the words that had been given him, turning them into such sweet music that the abbess became convinced that he had been called by God to another way of life. So she persuaded him to become a monk and received him into the minster, and bade the wise among the company teach him the words of the Bible, so that he might sing the Scriptures and thus bring greater glory to their religion.

Caedmon listened to the accounts from the Bible and turned them all into song, so that a great part of the Scriptures became known to the people of that community through his singing, which was so unlike anything that had ever been heard before that he was looked upon as being especially endowed with the divine favor.

Caedmon lived in the monastery until he became an old man, loved by all the Order and the people of the neighborhood, and his fame spread abroad throughout all England, and many strangers came to Whitby, attracted only by the wonder of his voice. The monks wrote his songs down carefully, and they were learned by all the people, and became as familiar as the war-songs and love-ballads that were sung at their feasts. And though many other minstrels tried to sing of heavenly things and rival Caedmon, they could not, for his gift was the greater, and was considered by all to be divine from the manner of its coming to him. So his fame remained unrivalled, and after many years death came to him at last as the monks were singing nocturns, and so he had sweet music till the end.

Without accepting the miraculous part of this tradition we may easily see how the idea of paraphrasing the Scriptures may have come to Caedmon in a dream; and it has been conjectured that his never having sung before was due to religious scruple, fostered by the missionaries, against encouraging the warlike and unchristian feelings aroused by the minstrelsy of the time, and that he used his native gift as soon as he conceived the idea of singing the praises of religion with it. He was deeply religious, he lived where there had been the greatest mingling of the British and Saxon races, and though we cannot say positively that he was of Celtic blood, it is certain that he was inspired by the Celtic and missionary spirit, and was hostile to the traditions of the Saxon bards, who celebrated the victories of their chiefs and the deeds of Norse heroes.

Although the subjects of his verse were not original with him, yet in his Paraphrase Caedmon showed himself a true poet, at a time when the English race was considered almost as barbarian by the more enlightened nations. The literature of any other country was quite unknown to him, and it is from this fact that his poetry is peculiarly valuable, since we are sure that whatever beauty it possesses belongs to Caedmon alone.

Besides their literary value, his works are important because of the influence they exerted over the English nation at a time when all books were written in Latin, and Caedmon's verse alone could reveal to the unlearned both the glory of the new faith and the possible beauty that had lain theretofore almost unrevealed in their own language.

CHAPTER IV.

THE VENERABLE BEDE.

One day, in the latter part of the seventh century, there came to St. Peter's Monastery at Wearmouth, a little boy of seven to be admitted to the school as a pupil. The good monk who entered his name little dreamed that the child before him was destined to become so famous that his fame would one day spread to all the learned nations. But such was the fact, for the boy was no other than the young Bede, who stands at the head of the early English writers. In those days the only schools in England were attached to the monasteries, as education was not common, and few of the people knew how to read and write. Such a state of igno-rance was considered no disgrace, for the English race at that time was busy about things that were then of much more importance than studying from books, for they were building a nation, and trying to make a united people out of many different elements.

And so the men who were quick in thought, brave in action, and resolute in will, were the most needed in England at that time, and very little attention was paid to books. The noble and wealthy classes were as unlearned as the peasants, and many a king ruled over the English nation who could not even write his name. Learning was almost entirely confined to the monks, whose profession kept them away from war, and whose peaceful lives held some chance for study.

But although kings, nobles, and peasants were alike thus ignorant of the knowledge that may be had from books, they were by no means unappreciative of the learning of others. They held knowledge in great esteem, and many a haughty earl who could command obedience from an army by a look, would bow in honest admiration and deference before some passing priest, whose murmured blessing seemed all the more valuable because delivered in Latin, the language of the learned.

The monasteries were generously endowed, and the schools attached to them were presided over often by scholars who were not unknown among the learned of other nations; and so it was possible even then to get what was considered a good education in England, though it was a rare thing to devote one's life to it.

School life in the monastery was for the most part pleasant, and the children and youths who lived there as pupils could not have had better training for the part they were to play in after-life. The monks were unselfish, truly pious, and often learned, and the example of their kindness to the poor and sick, in an age when strength was the law of life, could not but exert a noble influence on their pupils.

In these schools the pupil combined the study of books with various offices performed for the monks, and the young student would often be summoned from his books to ring the bell for prayers, or give alms to some beggar, or perhaps to take part in the reception of some noble whose gifts to the monastery commanded respectful and loyal attention for himself and his retinue.

Bede, entering Wearmouth at the age of seven, could have known very little of life outside the walls of St. Peter's, and as just at that time a more active interest than ever was excited in education, it is no wonder that the child easily imagined that learning was the chief thing in life, and even at that early age gave signs of the unusual brilliancy of his mind. With the other pupils he sang the offices of the church, performed the household duties required, worked in the gardens and fields with the monks, and gave his share of attention to the visitors at the monastery; but his heart was really bound up in his studies, and he found true pleasure only in them.

At that time a book meant simply a written copy of a manuscript, that was perhaps itself a copy, and all the writings of the ancients, or the works of those who were then living, were only preserved in this way. The writing was done on parchment made of the skins of goats, deer, or sheep, the leaves being sewed together and the covers made of boards. As the parchment was prepared by a slow and careful process,

4

only the most perfect pieces being used, and the manuscripts were copied by hand, the making of a book was very slow work. And as this work was done entirely by the monks and their pupils, only assisted sometimes by laymen who resided in the monastery, it came about very naturally that the monasteries held all the libraries in England. Some monasteries were very rich in books, possessing five hundred or a thousand; others had often only twenty or thirty. In every monastery there was a room called the Scriptorium, which was set apart for the making of books, and here the monks and their assistants worked diligently. The utmost care was taken to copy the text exactly, and the alteration of the shape of a single letter could not take place without the consent of the abbot. Sometimes it happened that a monk had won such a reputation for carefulness and workmanship, that he would be allowed to copy in his own cell, but more often all the work was done in the Scriptorium.

It is an easy thing to call up a picture of one of these old rooms, and see the workers seated at their desks, bending over their work with loving care, the silence broken only by an occasional footfall in the corridors outside, and the sombre colors of the monastic habits brightened by the white tunics and fresh young faces of the pupils.

And the actual copying was not the only element in book-making, for, not content with copying the exact words of the authors, the monks followed the examples of the ancients in making their manuscripts as beautiful as possible, by adorning the margins with illustrations, and introducing initial letters of intricate and graceful designs. The illustrations were done in gold leaf and brilliant water-colors, and the parchment was often colored in violet to enhance the effect. Nearly every page of the manuscript would contain some specimen of the illuminator's art, and the English and Irish monks won such a reputation for beautiful work in this regard, that other nations were glad to learn from them. Pictures in green, purple, gold, blue, and silver, flashed from the pages, either illustrating some incident mentioned in the chapter, or showing only the exquisite fancy of the illuminator, who was able in this way to prove and cultivate his love of the beautiful.

The pages so illuminated were deemed worthy of beautiful binding, and we find that the wooden lids were covered with leather or velvet, and adorned with jewels and designs in metal, the clasps being of gold and silver. Plainer volumes were tied by thongs of leather. Copies of the Bible, books of prayer, and legends of the saints were most frequently made, though the Greek and Latin classics and books of poetry, history, and romance were also sometimes copied.

Thus we see that a monk's life in those old days held a great many interests outside of religious matters, and as young Bede had early decided to give his life to study, and since all the books were found in the monasteries, it is not strange that he remained in a monastery all his life, going when he was ten years old from Wearmouth to the just finished convent of Yarrow, where he lived the rest of his days. His learning included every branch of knowl-

edge that was then known, and we have only
to look at his writings to see how far the world
had advanced in his time. He wrote principally in Latin, for in that way he was sure of
having his works understood by all learned
men, as Latin was the language of scholars all
over the world.

Although his books on theology, science, and
grammar showed his acquaintance with the wisdom of all ages, and won for him a great reputation at the time, it is his history of England
that has given him his place in English literature, for it is to this book that we owe more
than to any work that was written for hundreds
of years after. Bede called it the *Ecclesiastical
History of England*, because his real purpose
was to write the history of Christianity in England; but as at that time the history of the
Church was the history of the people, the work
is invaluable because of the information in regard to the growth of the nation, and its pictures of the every-day life of the people. It
was written in Latin, and in its pages are found
recorded all the events of national interest up

to his time. It is here, indeed, that we read the story of Caedmon's life, and it is perhaps due to this fact alone that the old poet was not utterly forgotten. But Bede enshrined Caedmon's song in the pages of his History as carefully and lovingly as one picks the first spring flower, and thus the earliest note of English poetry comes to us still as clear and sweet as when Caedmon sung it in the aisles of Whitby Chapel.

As his History was the most important, it was also almost the last effort of his life, for after it was finished he undertook no great work, but spent his last years content with the usual routine of a monk's duties. There was one service, however, which he wished to render to those who could not read his Latin treatises, for although he was one of the most learned men of the age he was still an Englishman, and had a loyal interest in the common people.   Therefore he desired to translate some portion of the Bible into the mother-tongue, and chose for this purpose the Gospel of St. John, thinking no doubt that this message of love would be understood by all.

We can see him then, in his old age, seated in the Scriptorium which he had first entered as a child, surrounded by his pupils, who gave him a love far beyond the common affection, and reading perhaps in their young faces the same eager hope that had filled his own breast when, as a novice, he had looked upon those treasured volumes, and sighed for the wisdom that lay between their jewelled covers.

The work of translation would have been an easy one to such a scholar as Bede, even though the language of the people was not yet perfectly formed, but he was old and enfeebled by sickness, and had it not been for the love he felt toward it he must have given up the task from very weakness. But he persevered, dictating day after day to his pupils, and only pausing when suffering compelled him to. He grew weaker as the work proceeded, and one day, feeling that the end was near, called his helpers to him and bade them write quickly, for he did not know how much time would be given him. And as the day wore on his strength failed so rapidly that his assistants feared the task was too great, and one of them said: "Most dear master, there is still one chapter left; do you think it troublesome to be asked more questions?" But Bede answered, "It is no trouble, write on." And so, with some intervals of resting, the day passed, and they were still at the task when, as the dusk gathered, the same pupil said, "Dear master, there is one sentence yet not written." And again Bede answered, "Write quickly." And when the boy had finished, we are told that Bede laid his head in his hands and, saying the Gloria, departed to the heavenly kingdom.

It is recorded by the monks that the title venerable, which is always attached to the name of Bede, was given by an angel who bent over the brother who had fallen asleep while writing his master's epitaph, and supplied a missing word. And the legend well illustrates the love and esteem in which he was held by the monks, who thought no honor too high to be paid to the beloved master whose presence had crowned their monastery with enduring fame.

CHAPTER V.

About a hundred years after the death of
Bede, which occurred in 735, a little prince was
born in England whose name was in time to be
as celebrated as that of the great teacher.

This was Alfred, son of Ethelwulf, king over
all England, and as the little prince was the
youngest of Ethelwulf's sons there was small
chance of his ever coming to the throne, even
in an age when the right of the eldest born was
often disputed. England at that time was in a
state of trouble that may well be compared to its
condition when invaded by the Saxons, and the
cause was of the same nature ; for a foreign foe
was again on the soil, and an enemy from across
the sea again threatened the land that had
known so much warfare.

These were the Northmen, a seafaring race

like the Saxons, called in England Danes, and
in France, where they also ventured, Normans,
and whose custom it was to descend upon any
foreign shore, murder the inhabitants, burn the
houses, and carry away captives and treasures,
just because they liked the excitement of adventure and the wealth and power it brought them.
The coasts of France and England were their
favorite places of resort, and the dwellers by
the sea had learned to regard the visits of these
marauders with horror, and shrunk from them
with a dread that was considered no shame;
for England was honestly trying, in the midst of
many domestic quarrels, to become a peaceable,
law abiding, and civilized nation, and the Danes,
who, when away from home on these maraud-
ing expeditions, laughed at law, despised peace,
and found pleasure in burning churches and
plundering monasteries, were rightly thought
the enemies of all progress in civilization.

For nearly a hundred years they had harried
England, and the people were never sure of
peace for a month at a time. Sometimes they
were defeated, sometimes they were bribed

with gold to depart in peace, sometimes after a successful raid they would go off of their own accord to plunder other places, but one never knew when they might not return; and, as after a while they not only came, but declared they had come to stay, the English found that the matter was very serious, and that, if England was to remain the land of the English, the Danes must be driven away utterly, or else held in such fear that they would be content to stay in the country without fighting for the control of it.

So the wars went on more fiercely than ever, and neither side could be said to win, for although the Danes did not conquer England, neither were they driven away, and the whole land was full of trouble because of their presence.

Little Prince Alfred was born just at a time when the contest was at its fiercest, and his earliest recollections were connected with the dreadful deeds committed by his country's enemies, and his heart was thrilled with horror many a time as he listened to the story of their terrible outrages against the lives and property of the English. At his father's court the high-est attention was paid to the training that would fit men for soldiers and military leaders to fight the Danes, and Alfred was taught to ride and fence as soon as he was old enough to sit a horse or hold a sword. And as he watched his father depart on some expedition against the Danes, and saw the white banner of the Saxons, with the figure of a horse embroidered upon it, floating proudly in the wind, he no doubt longed for the time when he too should follow that banner and be able to fight for his country.

The English court at that period was held with all the magnificence that could be com-manded, and the palaces of the king and no-bles were furnished with all the rare and costly articles that could be obtained. In the king's palace were golden tables, beautiful carved oaken chairs ornamented with beaten silver, tapestries and curtains of silk embroidered with gold and silver, and jewelled goblets from which the royal family drank their mead. Dress, too, received much attention, and the wealthy had garments of silk embroidered with golden flowers, and beautiful cloaks fastened with clasps of gold and silver, and set with precious stones. Rings were worn also, and heavy necklaces called neck-rings, and bracelets heavy and jewelled, and even the shoes were sometimes set with jewels. In the midst of such surroundings Alfred passed his early years, receiving such instruction as was common for a king's son, and profiting by it so well that at hunting, horse-racing, hawking, leaping, running, wrestling, and all other games, he easily outstripped his companions and showed the true qualities of a leader.

But, although he was thus accomplished in all the things that were then deemed necessary for the education of a prince, there were many others which interested him, for he was a thoughtful boy and keen-sighted, and very little escaped his observation. Among other things he pondered much over the beautiful books which he saw in the monasteries, or which were chained to a table in the halls of the palace; and, as he studied the pictures and lingered

over the exquisite illuminations, he often wondered how it would seem to be able to read,
and find out what the stories were about; for,
although he was expected to grow up and be a
great prince, it was not thought necessary that
he should be taught to read, for, why should
he learn to read when it would not help him to
govern? And in all England then there was
scarcely a noble who knew one letter from another.

Many a time, as Alfred sat in the hall of feasting and listened to the Saxon gleemen singing
of Beowulf and other heroes, or heard some
wandering Irish minstrel chant the old songs
of Taliesin, he felt a great wish to be able to
open the wonderful volumes that he had seen,
and perhaps find in them other stories as fascinating as those he was listening to. But this
could not be, and the only thing he could do
would be to go to the queen's apartment sometimes, and beg her to read to him out of the
books whose treasures seemed more inacces-
sible to him than fairyland. Once, as he was
bending over his mother while she read to him,

and admiring the beautiful book, she told him
that it should be the property of whichever of
the four brothers should first be able to read it.
The other princes cared nothing for this promise, and smiled to think of a Saxon prince bending over a book like a monk; but to Alfred the
words brought the fairest hope he could have
had.

He set himself about learning to read with
the same eagerness that had made him famous
among his companions as a wrestler and runner,
and in a short time, considering the difficulties
that lay in the way, he was able to call the
beautiful book his own.   And then it seemed
to him that the things he had known before
could not be compared with the knowledge that
might now be his, and his new gift was held as
precious as the magician's wand that could open
vast treasure-houses at the master's touch.

Alfred's love for music was great, and he was
a skilled player on the harp, and knew by heart
all the old songs that the harpers sang; but
from the time that he learned to read he began
to look at life more seriously than he had ever

done before, and he felt that there were other things in life than war, and hunting, and pleasure, and that a nation, to arrive at true greatness, must believe this. But although his knowledge of books went far toward forming his character, he had other advantages which were denied generally even to the sons of kings.

His father Ethelwulf had sent an expedition to visit Rome, which Alfred accompanied, though at the time he was only five years old, and thus he learned early that his own country was only a small portion of the world, and that a Saxon King, though brave in battle and strong in governing his country, might still have much to learn from nations whose greatness did not depend entirely upon the sword. Ethelwulf, on a second expedition to Rome, took Alfred with him again, and as the boy saw the costly presents—consisting of silver dishes, golden images, silken robes, a jewelled sword, and a crown of pure gold weighing four pounds—which his father gave to the Pope, he was again impressed with the idea that greatness included other things than personal courage or strength;

for, as a mark of favor, the Pope promised Ethelwulf that thereafter no Saxon should ever be
bound with iron bonds in Rome; and no soldier in Rome would have dared to disobey that
order, though it came from one who had never
carried a sword or stood on a field of battle.

By the time he was seventeen, Alfred was
considered the most promising of all of Ethelwulf's sons, and he had already seen more than
one battle with the Danes, who were as full of
determination as ever to conquer England.
More than once they had promised peace and
signed treaties, but the English had learned
that the word of a Dane could not be trusted,
and the land was as full of trouble as ever.

When Ethelwulf died he was succeeded in
turn by his three elder sons, who all fought the
Danes, and when Alfred came to the throne, in
his twenty-third year, he knew that hard work
lay before him. The year before his accession
he fought in eight battles against the enemy,
and yet peace seemed as far off as ever. For
six or seven years the war went on, in the old
ways, the Danes sometimes suing for peace,

5

sometimes gaining victories, and sometimes accepting money for their promise to go away; and toward the latter part of this time the English had become so disheartened that it seemed to them they would lose their country in spite of their brave resistance; for their army had dwindled down to almost nothing, the whole country was overrun by the Danes, and King Alfred himself was a fugitive from his court, and was hiding with a few loyal followers among the marshes. But hope did not forsake the king even in such a sad plight, and he was resolved to make one more great effort to rid his country from the enemy.

Chief of the Danish sea-kings at that time was Guthrum, whose name was held in horror by all England because of his zeal in plundering towns, burning monasteries, and killing women and children. Alfred knew that there would be no peace for England so long as this great chief remained unconquered, and besides, there was a tradition among the English that Guthrum was not only the fiercest of the sea-kings, but also the noblest in character, and the least likely to dishonor his plighted word. So it would be a great thing for England if, by defeat or other means, Guthrum could be made to consent to peace, and Alfred determined to bring this about if possible.

His camp, in the midst of wide marshes, was unknown to the enemy, who only knew that the Saxons were in hiding somewhere; for it was the habit of the king's men to sally forth from the camp and fall upon any small bands of Danes that might be passing near, and after a skirmish in which the Saxons were generally victorious, carry off provisions and arms to the king. The camp was well secured from intrusion by the nature of the soil, and so expert did the English become in harassing the enemy, that the Danes learned to look for a lurking Saxon in every clump of alder, or group of willows that fringed the streams which encircled the little island where Alfred had made his dwelling-place.

The Saxons for miles around knew the secret, but they kept it well, and it was not generally known even among themselves that it was the king who was at the head of the camp. But they learned that they could still trust the honor and courage of their king, even though he was a fugitive and slept in a hut made of logs and rushes instead of the royal palace.

And so, when the time came for action, the king found that the English, as a nation, were still loyal to him and their homes, and he had not much trouble in getting together an army. Messengers were sent from city to city and village to village, bearing the naked sword and arrow, the symbols of war, and the Saxons responded with right good will, giving the messenger God speed, and promising help when the time came. Then every Saxon heart thrilled again with hope, and at night every eye watched for the signal for action.

There is a story in the old histories which says that, in order to see the Danish camp, Alfred made up his mind to visit it himself rather than send any messenger, no matter how reliable or sharp-sighted he might be. Accordingly, he disguised himself as a wandering minstrel, and taking his harp, approached the

Danish camp and began to sing some of those old songs for which the gleemen were so famous. The Danish sentinels were glad enough to have the beautiful voice of the singer and the exquisite tones of his harp break in upon the monotony of their watch, and they encouraged him to sing song after song, and finally admitted him to the camp. Alfred passed from tent to tent, charming the soldiers with his music, and one of the chiefs was so pleased with his skill that he insisted on leading him into the presence of Guthrum himself.

And so the rival kings met face to face, and Guthrum, at whose name all England trembled, forgot for a while that he was a great warrior and that his chiefs were looking to him to conquer a nation, and listened to Alfred's singing, which no doubt brought up old memories of days in which warfare had no part. But although Alfred used his voice with such good effect, he did not forget that he had come there to use his eyes more, and when he left Guthrum's presence, loaded with the gifts that it was customary to bestow upon the gleemen, he bore away with him a very good idea of the Danish forces and resources, and could calculate pretty fairly how a battle might go.

And so, when he returned to his camp among the marshes, he called his chieftains together, and kneeling down under the great Saxon banner, drew on the ground, by the light of the torches, the plan of the Danish camp, and declared that the hour had come and he was ready to strike one more blow for English liberty. The signal spread from point to point, and such an army gathered that Alfred was able completely to surround the Danish camp, and repulse every attempt of the enemy to break through. At last, after a two weeks' siege Guthrum was willing to agree to peace and accept Alfred's offer of friendship, and his permission to remain in England so long as he respected the English nation's rights.

Guthrum was so impressed by Alfred's generosity to a conquered foe, that he did not find it difficult to believe him when told that this kindness to any enemy was taught by the Christian religion, which forbade making war for its own sake and commanded instead acts of mercy and forgiveness. And this doctrine, which was so powerfully preached by Alfred's conduct, seeming to Guthrum more noble than his own faith, be consented to be baptized, King Alfred becoming his sponsor; and as his army followed his example, the Danes in England were considered thenceforth as Christians.

The defeat of Guthrum was one of the most important events in early English history. It saved the English nation at the moment of its greatest peril, and helped the work of civilization, which must have been put back for a long period if the Danes had been successful. And, although Alfred had still much trouble from other bands of sea-kings who descended upon the coasts, and the Danes and Saxons did not trust each other fully for many years, the supremacy of the English remained in full force, and the country finally became so peaceful and law abiding, that it was said that golden bracelets might be hung upon the landmarks along the highways without fear of their being stolen.

Although this, of course, could not be true, it

may still illustrate the difference between the condition of the country then, and its state during the years when the Danes prowled around like hungry wolves, and no man could leave his home in the morning without the fear that when he returned at night he might find only the ruins left by the hands of a relentless enemy.

Outside of the saving of the nation and the comfort which peace brought, the defeat of the Danes had still another important and lasting effect upon the history of the people. And this was the preservation of the libraries, which enabled the progress of literature to continue uninterrupted. If Guthrum had really conquered England, and Alfred had been slain or forced into exile, there is little doubt that the Danes, following their usual custom when dealing with a conquered enemy, by destroying what was considered most precious, would have burned monasteries, destroyed books, and forced many scholars, both among priests and laymen, into exile in France or Italy.

Thus learning would have suffered greatly, and England would have been almost illiterate

again until such time as the two races had become one, and knowledge had been brought
from abroad. And this would have taken a
long time to accomplish, and the literature aris-
ing from such a state would have been quite
different in character from our early English
writings. But the Saxon gained the day, kept
the domestic arts, taught the Dane how to till
the ground and gather the harvest, build houses,
and respect the laws; and hardly had the first
flowers bloomed on the old battle-fields when
Alfred was busy again with his interrupted
studies, inviting scholars from abroad to his
court, and forming great plans to make an in-
telligent and educated people out of the rough
material he had to deal with.

His own love of learning was so strong that
he could not help but impart an interest in it to
others, and in order to make this interest more
active he founded schools which he ordered all
children to attend, and formed the plan of having the knowledge which was locked away in
Latin manuscripts brought to the reach of all by
having it translated into the common tongue.

His own work in this respect is the most important of the age, and he is no less famous as a scholar than as a king and warrior. His most important work was the translation of Bede's History. This being in Latin, was of course unfamiliar to the common people, and Alfred desired above all things that the history of the country should be known to all. He therefore transcribed the Latin into English, so that all who could read might become familiar with it, and learn the lessons which Bede tried to teach, that the true glory of a nation lay not in ceaseless war, but in cultivating the arts of peace; and that the names of mighty warriors, however brilliantly they might shine, would always be dim beside those which stood for noble manhood and the progress of the race. It was through this translation of King Alfred that the English people first became interested in their own history, and thus his service may be considered as equally valuable to his age with that of Bede, to whom succeeding generations have owed so much.

King Alfred also translated a book called the

Consolations of Philosophy, by Boethius, a Roman writer who lived some four hundred years before his time. Boethius wrote his great work while in prison on a charge of treason, which finally led to his death. The *Consolations* were written in five books, which taught that God ruled the world and was the source of all good, that even the most miserable of mankind can find comfort by fixing his mind on divine things, and that as seen from above only the good are happy. The Christian monks saw so much good in this work, which was written from the heart of one who had suffered the saddest experiences, that they regarded it as well worth their study, and valued it so highly that it was used almost daily in all schools and monasteries.

Another interesting translation by Alfred was that of the writings of Orosius, a Spanish monk who wrote a history of the world from the creation, and whose work was used as a text-book of history and geography in the schools. Although Orosius had lived in the fifth century, the knowledge of geography had not increased very largely since his time, and as Alfred desired to make additions to this part of the book, he sent messengers to various parts of the world to gather all the information they could about distant countries ; one of these em- bassies had even journeyed as far as India, and Alfred added the information they brought to the writings of Orosius. He also entertained at his court all the great travellers he could in- duce to come there, and listened to their de- scriptions of strange nations, and by adding the knowledge thus gained he gave the book a much greater value.

Travelling in those days, when there were no railroads or steamers, and when there was con- stant danger to life from man and beast, as well as from the perils of unfamiliar ways, was a thing seldom indulged in except from necessity, and the traveller was held in great honor always, as one of strange experiences who had had his courage tested in the sharpest way.

Two of the most celebrated travellers at that time were Wulfstan and Othere, who had travelled far north, and their fame reached the ear of Alfred, who invited them to England and heard their adventures from their own lips. Othere, who was a Norwegian, had sailed round the North Cape into the White Sea, and Wulfstan, who is supposed to have been a Jute, had ventured far north in the Baltic, and Alfred also added their accounts to the book of Orosius. Thus, when he finally gave the work into the hands of pupils of the school, it contained as accurate an account as it was possible to obtain of the geography of Europe at that time.

These translations, which held much of the knowledge that was then taught, being taken from their Latin dress and put into English, could still be used as text-books in the schools where English was being taught, and thus were of great importance.

But, besides these and other translations, Alfred will also be distinguished for his own wise laws, which secured such peace to the country and which were so just, that they can still be quoted as authority. And the love of liberty and justice can never be seen more clearly than in the life of this great man, whose power of command might easily have been put to the most tyrannical uses if he had so willed. His place in English literature is important, because he preserved books and learning at a time when civilization seemed to be passing away from the land, and his place in English history is equally important, because in an age when might so often made right, he proved that justice was greater than power, and forgiveness nobler than revenge. And so, whether as king, soldier, or scholar, his name must forever be connected with the first true progress of the English nation.

CHAPTER VI.

THE ROMANCE OF KING ARTHUR.

Alfred's efforts to keep England for the English could only preserve peace during his own life-time, and hardly had he died when the troubles began again, and king after king ascended the English throne to spend his life in fighting with the Danes. This lasted for a hundred years, and finally England was conquered by Swein, king of Denmark, and the Danes held the country for forty years. But after that the English gained the power again and held it for the next twenty-five years, during which time the Danes in England were brought nearer and nearer to their old enemies by ties of marriage and friendship, and by those common interests which must exist between two races living in the same country, however bitterly they might hate each other in the beginning;

and at last when Harold, the last English King, came to the throne, Danes and English considered themselves as one people, and were ready to stand by and fight for each other like brothers, if occasion demanded.

And it was well that this was so, for England was approaching a time in her history when she would need braver and truer hearts to defend her than she had ever needed before. Harold was the son of Godwin, once a Saxon peasant who began life as a cow-herd, but now the most powerful of the English earls, and although his mother had been a Dane, he felt himself only English, and was determined to bring back the lost splendor of the English crown. But he had for an enemy William, Duke of Normandy, who had long looked with covetous eyes on England, and whose strongest ambition it was to become the ruler of the island kingdom. He claimed that he had a right to the English throne because he was a cousin of Edward the Confessor, the last king before Harold.

Edward, called the Confessor because of his piety, had spent his early years at the Norman court, while a Danish king was still on the throne, and during that time he had learned the French language and had grown so fond of French customs that it was said by the English he was more Norman than Saxon. His subjects were bitterly jealous of the Norman favorites he always had around him, and longed for the time when they should be sent back to their own country. Harold's accession to the throne made the court English as well as the country, and the people were rejoiced at the change. But their joy was short, for no sooner had the news reached France than William of Normandy began to make preparations for the invasion of England. He offered to his noblemen the castles and lands of the Saxon earls, to the soldiers " good pay and the pillage of England," and his terms were eagerly accepted.

The Norman barons set to work with a will: armies were raised as if by magic, and ships were built, armor, lances, and swords forged, and banners embroidered with the emblems of the different lords who dreamed of the day when they should see them floating over the Saxon

6

castles. Numbers of men-at-arms in France and Germany flocked into Normandy and offered their services to the man who had promised them the booty they might make, and camp-followers polished armor and spurs, sharpened swords and spears, pikes and javelins, and waited impatiently for the hour when they might descend on the English coast.

England, unhappily, was threatened with other foes than the Normans at that time, for the king of Norway had landed on the northern coast and was ravaging it at the very time that Norman and Saxon met at Hastings, near where William had disembarked. On October 14, 1066, a battle was fought which proved one of the most memorable events in English history. The contest, which may be said to have begun with the song which the first advancing Norman sang as he rode forward and was met by a Saxon knight, raged the long day through, and at night Harold lay pierced through the brain with a Norman arrow, and the fate of the English throne was decided.

William the Norman, called in history the

Conqueror, was crowned at Westminster, and England became a land ruled by a foreign despot, who parcelled the country out to his favorites, made laws that best suited his own designs, and above all, ordered all business to be transacted in French, which he made the legal language in the hope that the people would be forced to use it and in time forget their mother tongue.   But the people refused to acknowledge William king in their hearts, though they were forced to do so outwardly.   And they cherished a desperate hope that fortune would again place the crown upon the head of a Saxon king.

This hope sustained them in those dark hours when they saw their homes taken from them and given to the Normans, and knew that justice existed only for their enemies.   And as William well knew the temper of the people, his reign was by no means a peaceful one, and he could only look forward to a dark future for the sons who were to reign after him.   The use of the French language at the court, in all schools, and in the halls of justice, together with the unsettled state of the country, had the most disastrous effect upon learning and literature. English lads who should have been studying in the schools were roaming about the forests, harboring only thoughts of revenge against the king they had been taught to hate, and as the Saxons were looked down upon by the Normans as an inferior race, even the clergy had little respect paid to them, no matter how learned they might be. Thus among the English people the love of learning which Alfred had tried to instil was gradually slipping away, for they chose to be ignorant rather than to get knowledge through the language of the foreigners that they hated. And it was only when the two races had become somewhat reconciled that it was possible for literature again to be looked upon with interest.

During the years which followed immediately after the conquest all books which were written —and as a rule it was only the clergy who wrote—were in Latin if they were prose, while the poetry and songs which the Normans brought with them from France were written in French. What is known as popular literature, the literature of the common people, did not exist in those days of violence and bloodshed ; for the Saxon, whether he were earl or peasant, could only think of defending his home from his enemies, and his dependents from the most cruel oppression.

But in the reign of William Rufus, the son of the Conqueror, an event occurred which so influenced the thought of the people that it gave rise in time to a new literature. This was the First Crusade, an expedition undertaken by the nations of Western Europe to recover the Holy Sepulchre at Jerusalem from the Turks, who were then ruling in Palestine. The Christian Church thought it a disgrace that the tomb of Christ should be in the possession of an infidel nation, and sermons were preached by the monks all over the Christian world, urging men to join the crusade. This appeal was responded to with such enthusiasm that hundreds of thousands of soldiers were soon on their way to Jerusalem, and from this time on, for nearly two hundred years, there was scarcely a period in which a crusade was not being carried on.

Sometimes the crusaders were successful, and sometimes their enemies, but the chief work of the crusades was after all, not the taking or keeping the Holy Sepulchre, but the effect that they had upon Western Europe. The French and English and German nations were brought into contact in the East with the Greeks and Arabs, two nations that were celebrated for their learning, and this had a great influence upon their civilization. Knowledge began to gain more friends, and out of the darkness which had settled over literature a light began to shine. In England this was especially true, and while the crusades were considered by many as chiefly beneficial because of the wealth that came to the country from commerce with other nations, the more thoughtful saw that contact with other civilizations was just the thing that was needed to bring out their own powers more fully, and turn their thoughts toward higher things than battle or conquest.

During the time to which the crusades belong the children of the nobility had a careful training, although books played a small part, for they were taught the customs and practices of chivalry. The education of a boy of gentle birth began in his seventh or eighth year, and was supposed to end only when he had obtained the honor of knighthood, which was usually conferred some time after he was twenty. The castles of the great barons were the schools in which these children were taught. Here would come the sons of the lesser nobles, with those of the class called gentle, who were not of necessity of noble blood ; while often would be found in the company the little son of one of the most powerful lords, who was sent there to be taught because his father was brother-in-arms to the chief of the castle. The pupils were called pages, and were taught the use of arms, horsemanship, strict obedience to their superiors, and courtesy to all women. Their training was strict and often severe, but developed that courage, grace, firmness, and gentleness which were supposed to belong to every true knight.

Sometimes in the same castle would be found also the daughters of the nobles and gentry, who were in charge of the lady of the castle, who had them taught embroidery, weaving, sewing, housewifery, and the care of the sick; and it often happened that a little page would be placed in attendance upon one of these young girls, and have for a part of his duties serving her in every way possible; for it was thought that in this way could be best taught those fine and gentle manners which characterized the age of chivalry.

The ceremonies which ended the education of a youth and admitted him to knighthood were very solemn and impressive, and could not fail to leave a mark on his character. On the eve of the day on which he was to be consecrated the candidate confessed his sins to the priest, and then kneeling before the altar, passed the night in prayer. In the morning, after mass, he laid his sword on the altar to signify that his life thereafter would be devoted to the service of the good, and after a benediction had been pronounced upon it he received it again. Then a slight blow was given him on the check or shoulder, as the last insult he should ever receive submissively.   Then followed the oath, in which the new knight promised to maintain the right, relieve the poor and distressed, and act on all occasions worthy of his knighthood.

This was the last act in the education of a youth in the days of chivalry, an institution which had such an influence over the minds of the nation that it is not strange to find that the deeds of knights, their wars, tournaments, adventures, always filled all hearts with the greatest interest, and made almost every act of life depend in some way or other upon them.

Following both the English and Norman customs, the deeds of chivalry were recounted and sung by minstrel and troubadour in the baronial halls, just as the Saxon gleeman had chanted the old war-songs in the mead-hall of his chief. The fondness of the Normans for story-telling was as great as that of the old Saxons, and they brought into England many stories of Roland and other popular heroes, which the people at large became familiar with as the years went on.   And although there were some great scholars among churchmen and lay-men who wrote learned books in Latin, yet the first popular book after the invasion of the Normans, the book which first took hold of the hearts of the people, dealt with the romance, the tales of adventure, and songs of love which were the literature of the age of chivalry.

The book was called the " History of the Britons," and was compiled probably about the year 1147, by a monk named Geoffrey, called in literature Geoffrey of Monmouth, because he was educated at, and afterward became a priest of, the monastery at Monmouth.

The first part of the book relates the history of Britain from the earliest times ; but it was the second part, which cannot properly be called history at all, which stirred the fancy of the people and made literature once more popular. Into this second part Geoffrey incorporated the more or less fabulous life and adventures of Arthur, king of the Britons, who represented in his person all the glory and nobility of knight-hood. And although its origin was in great measure due to Norman thought and manners, yet it was after all an English book, as it described English sights and scenes. The rivers and hills, the meadows and the birds that sang therein, the flowers by the wayside, the May day festivals, and even the bloody combats, were all English.

King Arthur, who was supposed to have lived in the sixth century, was a king of the Britons after they had been converted to Christianity. Geoffrey's story tells how Arthur's father, Uther, had a wonderful dream in which he saw a comet, one ray of which ended in a fiery dragon out of whose mouth proceeded two other rays of light, one reaching out over France and the other over Ireland; and the interpretation of the dream was that he should have a son whose power and glory should reach to the uttermost ends of the earth. Therefore, in remembrance of the dream Uther had two dragons made of gold, and one he gave to the cathedral at Winchester and the other he carried with him in all his wars, and gained many victories thereby, being called from that time Uther Pendragon. And when he came to the throne he ruled wisely, and fought many great battles in which he subdued the enemies of the land. And when the wars were over, wishing to raise a monument to the soldiers who had been slain in battle, he called together all his wise builders and told them of his design. But Merlin, the magician, hearing of this, came to the king and told him that a fitting monument would never be raised until they brought the Giants' Dance from Ireland.

Now, Merlin was the greatest magician in the world. Before the reign of Uther, and while another king ruled, he had come into the kingdom because the story of his skill had reached the court and the king was desirous of seeing him ; for he was in great trouble about a palace which he wished to build in a certain place, and which disappeared in the ground every evening after the workmen had gone home. The king's wise men said that this would continue to be so until the ground was sprinkled with the blood of Merlin, who was then living in a distant place ; but when Merlin came into the presence of the king, he astonished the court so by his wisdom that it was at once seen that he was greater than all the magicians present. He told the king that the ground swallowed up the palace every night because underneath it was a magic pool, over which were two hollow stones each holding a sleeping dragon. And the king ordered his men to dig down into the ground, and they found that it was just as Merlin had said. One of the dragons was red and the other white, and as soon as they were released from the stones they began a furious battle, and the scene was so terrible that even the bravest warriors dreaded to look upon it.

And when the king asked what this signified, Merlin prophesied a wonderful prophecy, and foretold all the events that would happen to that kingdom through all future time. The prophecy related the after-glory of Britain, but it was also so full of coming woes that it terrified the people even more than the battle of the dragons; for Merlin foretold how the rivers would be turned to blood, and the fruits of the trees to ashes, how the cities would vanish in a night, and how a great serpent, whose length was coiled around the whole island, would work dreadful destruction upon the inhabitants, and how even the stars would change their places in the sky and bring great evils upon the land.

From this time the greatest honor was paid to Merlin, who remained at the court and in the time of Uther was still considered the greatest of magicians, whose advice must always be followed. And so, when he told Uther to have the Giants' Dance brought from Ireland, the king was greatly puzzled, for it seemed an impossible and yet necessary thing to do.

The Giants' Dance was an immense structure on top of a lofty mountain in Ireland, and was built of magic stones which had been brought from the farthest coast of Africa when giants inhabited the land. These stones were formed into a huge bath and possessed such healing properties, that whoever should step into the water they enclosed would be cured of all diseases. And although many pilgrimages were made thither by those who wished to see them, yet it would have been counted as easy to move the mountain itself as the mighty structure which it held, for the people were entirely ignorant of the mechanical arts by which such things were done. But as Merlin insisted, Uther sent an army of workmen into Ireland who honestly tried to move the stones, though ropes and cables were as ineffectual as silken threads would have been, and it was only when Merlin used magic that the deed was done. And so the Giants' Dance was removed and was set up as a monument for the dead, and was considered the greatest marvel that had ever been known in Britain.

On his father's death Arthur came to the throne, being in his fifteenth year, and then we have the account of the battles he fought, and of the great deeds he accomplished, and are told that in one battle he slew over four hundred men with his own sword. And then is related the story of his coronation, in the City of Legions, known now as Caerleon on the Usk, which the book says was washed on one side by the beautiful river, and was chosen for the coronation because the kings and princes from across the sea might have the pleasure of sailing right up to the city without leaving their ships. On the side away from the river, we are told, Caerleon was beautiful with meadows and groves, and the magnificence of its royal palaces, with lofty gilded roofs, made it rival even Rome, which was considered the most magnificent city in the world. We also read about the great rejoicing and gay festivities that signalized the event, and see Arthur in his coronation robes, preceded by four kings each bearing a golden sword, and accompanied by Queen Guenever bearing four white doves, on his way to the cathedral, where he was crowned with great solemnity, the ceremony being accompanied by music of such exquisite harmony that the like had never been known before.

Then follow the adventures of Arthur with neighboring and foreign powers, and at last we have an account of the treachery of Mordred, a kinsman whom Arthur left in charge of his kingdom while away on a foreign war, and who basely seized the kingdom for his own. And then comes the story of the last battle fought by Arthur, in which there was such slaughter as no battle-field had ever seen before. But although Mordred was slain, Arthur likewise received his death-wound, and was borne away by unknown hands to the vale of Avallon, and his people saw him no more.

Geoffrey's book ends here, but later on the story of Arthur included many other strange adventures, and tells how he founded the Round Table, that glorious company of knights whose deeds were recounted all over the civilized world, and of the wonderful deeds which Arthur accomplished with his sword Excalibar, which shone so when it was brandished that it gave a light equal to thirty torches, and blinded the eyes of all who looked upon it. For it was a magic sword, and Arthur had received it from a hand which rose up from the waters of a mystic lake, and was assured that no harm could come to him so long as he kept the scabbard safe.

And then there are descriptions of tournaments and journeys and adventures of all kinds,

7

all written in such a way that the reader could almost see the figure of Arthur, taller than other men, in his magnificent armor, and Excalibar flashing lightnings all around, and beautiful Guinevere (or Guenever, as Geoffrey calls her) his queen, and the ladies of the court, and the brave knights, and the great hall of the Round Table with its costly and splendid adornments, and the Round Table itself, surrounded by seats on which were written the names of the knights in letters of gold, and all the strange and wonderful scenes which belonged to that knightly court.

And these later stories relate that after Arthur had received his mortal wound in battle with Mordred, he was carried away by three queens to the vale of Avallon to be cured of his wound, when he would come again to rule over Britain. This tradition remained among the people for hundreds of years, and old legends relate that many times the foresters saw at noontide, or under the full moon, mounted knights flitting through the trees, and heard the sound of horns and the baying of hounds, and knew that it was Arthur and his knights of the Round Table out hunting; and so general was this belief among all the nations who heard the romance of Arthur that it was universally believed he would return; and far away in Sicily the peasants claimed that they could see at twilight the mystic vale of Avallon shining through the dusk, and the palace where Arthur had been borne to be cured of his wounds.

These later stories, which were written after the appearance of Geoffrey's book, and which also contained the stories of the knights of the Round Table, made the story of Arthur more complete, but the great credit belongs to Geoffrey of Monmouth of first presenting the stories in such a way as to win immediate popular favor. Geoffrey wrote his book in Latin, asserting that he had translated it from an old book of British tales, but it won such favor that it was translated into Norman French by Wace, a writer of popular romances, who added a continuation connecting the British with the ancient Trojans. In this form, and in the original form as written by Geoffrey of Monmouth, it was the favorite book of the nobility and all educated people. During this time of its great popularity, it was in the reign of King John put into English verse, like that of Beowulf, by Layamon, a priest at Ernley in Worcestershire, who doubled the length of Wace's form of the poem by adding what he knew of West Country tradition. The story, as told by Layamon, was incorporated in his translation of Geoffrey of Monmouth's Chronicle of Britain, and was called *Layamon's Brut*, and is very important because it contains the fullest account of the traditional history of Britain. Besides these forms of the poem, with the Trojan legends, there was still another version which has had a great influence on English thought, and that was the Christianized and moral form of the Arthurian legends made by Geoffrey of Monmouth's friend and contemporary, Walter Map. Map added the beautiful legend of *The Holy Graal*, and the spirit of his version is continued in our own day by *The Idyls of the King*, of Tennyson.

And although many doubts were cast upon

the truth of these romances, and the writer was censured for giving as history what was believed to be only legend, yet the book was read by old and young, far and near, with the greatest delight, and became such a favorite that for a time no other book was so much read; and old authors relate that he who was ignorant of it was considered to be no more accomplished than a clown. But its greatest value in literature is the influence which it had upon succeeding writers—an influence which has not yet died out, and to which we owe some of the masterpieces of English literature. And that the romance of King Arthur as we have it now, with the stories of Lancelot, Percival, Galahad, and all the great company of the Round Table, is much more complete and beautiful than the book of Geoffrey, does not in the least detract from the value of the old story which thrilled the hearts of the people for whom it was written, and made books and bookmen more popular in England than any other book that had been written since the Conquest.

CHAPTER VII.

ROBIN HOOD : THE HERO OF THE PEOPLE.

Besides the stories of Arthur and his knights, the English songs during the century following the Conquest also included the ballads of Robin Hood, a popular hero about whom numerous songs were composed, both during his life and later on. These ballads represented the feeling of the people as the stories of Arthur did those of the nobility. Robin Hood and people of his class rose naturally from the condition of society during those years; for, while the Norman barons were taking possession of England, dividing the land among themselves and building hundreds of castles all over the country, not only did the dispossessed nobility suffer, but the common people, the Saxon and Danish peasants, many of whom had been driven from their homes, or forced into a condition almost like slavery, were also falling into a way of life that had been almost unknown in England before the Conquest.

One of the first acts of William the Norman had been the setting apart of great tracts of forest lands for his own hunting grounds.   And not content with this, he even destroyed villages and laid waste farms in order that the land thus obtained might be planted with trees and made fit for the habitation of the deer and other animals which he loved to chase.   These royal forests were under the protection of the king himself, and the laws concerning them were among the strictest of the realm, for William loved hunting next to fighting, and considered one tree of more value than the lives of a dozen Saxon peasants.

Each forest was divided up into different portions called walks, which were in charge of keepers and their assistants, and there were as many rules and regulations to be observed as in the management of the court itself.   The royal foresters wore a certain uniform, or livery, which was recognized everywhere, and demanded the same respect as was shown to other officers of the king ; and in fact, the deference which they received was really greater than that paid to an officer of the court, for the foresters had to deal directly with the people, and life and property were often taken from the peasant who dared to offend one of these keepers.

The foresters went their rounds at stated times, and then woe to the unlucky person who should be caught transgressing the forest rules, which were so numerous that it was almost impossible to remember them. All persons found walking through the forests followed by dogs were subject to arrest, unless the dogs were held in leash. Every man who wore a cloak, under which might be concealed weapons, was also liable to arrest. No man might even enter the forest carrying a bow, unless the string were first detached. If a poor peasant went there to cut a few pieces of turf or peat for his fire, he must do it at night or in the dusk, and in this manner try to escape the eye of the officer, who would have taken him to prison for the offence ; while the setting of a trap was looked upon as the greatest crime, even though the king had reduced the peasants to a condition of beggary by his cruel laws.

Thus the foresters and the peasants were at open warfare all the time, and each class tried its best to outwit the other. The lives of the keepers depended upon their fidelity to the king, and the peasants would never acknowledge that the Norman had any right to English property, and considered that they were doing a meritorious act if they could bring down a bird, wound a deer to the death, and secrete it in some hidden place where they might come at night and bear it away, or snare some of the smaller game which was so abundant. And, considering the vigilance of the officers, this happened pretty often, and still more often the offender escaped and was able to tell a merry tale of the adventure to the gay company seated around the fire, waiting for the feast which the busy housewife was preparing, and which would be enjoyed all the more because the viands were obtained in such a manner.

And after a while, as the oppression increased,

and the times seemed to grow worse instead of better, the people became even more daring and lawless; for the poverty of the people was bitter, and often there was only a choice of death by starvation or the chance of death by the law; and they chose the latter, and made daring expeditions into the forests, while the king and his keepers were at their wits' end to find ways of bringing the transgressors to justice. This was, indeed, hard to do. Outside of the forests stood the halls of the barons, frowning from some height, or commanding wide stretches of pleasant country, and never far away could be seen the convents, and both castle and convent were held by Norman influence and were friendly to the king. But away from these lived the great mass of people who loved to call themselves Saxon, and who felt themselves the rightful owners of the soil, though they lived in huts with mud walls and thatched roofs, and were often hungry, and always oppressed. And in spite of his mighty army, and his servile courtiers, and fawning priests, William found that he could not really conquer this Saxon people whose ignorance he despised and laughed at; and although he stole their lands, and denied them justice of every kind, he knew that their spirit was still unsubdued, and he could no more conquer it than he could control the wind or the waves.

And what troubled him most was that his beautiful forests, that he had laid out and protected with such care, should be the cause of the greatest annoyance of all. For he could no more keep the Saxons out than he could keep the birds out, and he knew that the very game that he watched so carefully was looked upon as lawful spoil by the peasants, who enjoyed it more often than he did himself.

From occasional visits to the forests, the people came gradually to form the habit of staying there longer, and many a little camp was made in the deep woods, and many a merry company gathered there unsuspected by the foresters. These camps were principally formed of men who had transgressed the law in some way, for the Saxon's chief refuge in time of trouble was the fens and woods, which he knew by heart. The Norman laws, so strict and numerous, were constantly being broken by the peasants, either intentionally or unintentionally, and then, as they knew they could get no justice from the law, they would flee to the fens or forests and feel moderately safe, knowing that so long as they kept away from the highway or open country the king's officers would have a hard time to find them.

These refugees gradually formed themselves into bands, having separate hiding-places which were known only to friends, and as time went on these companies became so large that they were very formidable to deal with; for they no longer kept close to the forest, but would venture out into the highway or surrounding country, terrifying travellers and demanding money and alms. These bands were called highwaymen and robbers by the Normans, but the Saxons called them the merry men of the greenwood, and were proud of their exploits, and were always ready to shelter them in their homes, and protect them by misleading the officers who were in search of them.

This life became so popular that the outlaws were regarded almost with envy by their soberer-minded countrymen. Every family almost could boast of some relative or friend who had taken to life in the greenwood, and every fireside was familiar with the tales of the daring adventures of the merry men, while the deeds they did, and the songs they sang, became a part of the history of the time. These bands of adventurers held their own in the king's forests for so many years, that they came to be regarded almost as a necessity, and as time went on the bands were recruited; and at last, when the original outlaws had all died, the place they had made was still filled by other bold spirits, and thus, for over a hundred years the royal forests were held to be the lawful homes of these adventurers.

One of the boldest of the merry men was Robin Hood, who is supposed by some to have lived during the reign of Henry the Second, the grandson of the conqueror, though others assert that he lived at a much later time. It is almost as hard to find out the dates of this period as to give the exact date for the birth of Taliesin or King Arthur, but the important thing to know is, that Robin Hood was, in all probability, a real hero and the chief of the merry men, and to remember that the songs and ballads which relate to him and his gay company have an important place in English literature; for it was while the songs of Robin Hood were being sung that the English nation was incorporating with it the Norman element. A new language was gradually being formed, and thus its legends in regard to the merry men give us true pictures of the lives of the people at that time.

And just as in the stories about King Arthur we learn how the great barons and knights lived, and see them in their wars, and at the tournament and chase, and in the halls of the castle, so in the legends of Robin Hood and the men of the greenwood we see the life of the common people, and hear their songs and see their games; and both pictures are equally interesting and important, for both tell us, as nothing else can, the life of those far off times

when the knight lived one life and the peasant
another, so different that it hardly seems that
they could have belonged to the same race.
Therefore, whether Robin Hood was born in
the year 1160, as some books say, matters little, for whenever he was born he stands for a
type of a class that represented the Saxon during the time of Norman power, and as such he
is of the greatest value. The same authority
that gives 1160 as his birth, says also that he
was of noble blood, and could have claimed a
title if he had wished.

But this also matters little, for his life was
that of the common people, however noble his
birth, and he liked no title so well as that which
made him prince of the Merry Men of the Greenwood. The particular place that he chose for
his exploits was Sherwood Forest, one of the
royal forests, and forever after celebrated as
the scene of most of his adventures. Here he
lived with a hundred brave spirits as bold as
himself, and the deeds that he did speedily
made him a favorite with the common people,
while his name was equally dreaded by the

king and nobles ; for Robin Hood knew no re-spect for rank, and would have stopped even the king himself on the highway, and demanded largess for himself and band, and alms for the poor and sick ; for he was the kindest-hearted highwayman, and devoted a good share of his plunder to the unfortunate peasants.

His band consisted of a hundred picked men, all skilful archers, and so celebrated that no force dare attack them unless they were out-numbered at least four times. Some of these men were so renowned that their names are as well known as that of Robin Hood himself, who took great pride in his band, and it was said would never receive a new member until he had fought a round with him and had tested his mettle.

Chief among the band was the celebrated Little John, who received his name, it is said, from his great stature, and who is also some-times called John Nailor. Little John was Robin Hood's chief counsellor and reliance always, and of all the band was the one who approached most nearly to the character of Robin Hood himself. In many ways he was said to rival the great chief, and in his use of the bow he was considered his equal. Hundreds of years after the merry men of Sherwood Forest had passed away, there were still shown at Whitby Abbey two pillars which, it was said, had been set up in commemoration of Robin Hood and Little John, who on a visit to the Abbot sent their arrows a mile away from the abbey, in order to show their host what fine archers they were. As Robin Hood boasted more of his archery than of any other accomplishment, it may be easily seen from this how Little John would be his prime favorite; for Robin Hood loved best the men whom he found it hardest to outshine in the games and sports and adventures which made up the life in the forest.

Another celebrated member of the band was Will Scarlet, whom tradition says Robin Hood bound to him by the strongest ties; for meeting Scarlet in the woods and finding him low-spirited and forlorn, because his promised wife had been taken from him by her parents and given to another suitor, Robin Hood promised him help, collected his band, descended upon the village just as the wedding-bells were ringing, and in a short time, much to the astonishment of the company, had the marriage ceremony performed with Scarlet for the bridegroom, and thus won his faith and gratitude forever. Among other favorites of Robin Hood were also George à Green; Pinder, whose name signifies that he was a pound-keeper; Much, a miller's son; and Friar Tuck, a jolly monk who, for some reason or other, preferred the life in Sherwood Forest to one in a convent, and whose exploits are almost as famous as those of the celebrated leader himself.

With this congenial fellowship, Robin Hood spent merry days in the forest, hunting the king's deer, keeping the royal foresters in constant dread of his pranks, and issuing forth into the highway at times to gather spoils from luckless travellers. But although he and his band were outlaws, and had a price set upon their heads, they were such general favorites that the whole of England might have been a shelter to them in time of trouble; for, far beyond Sherwood Forest had their renown spread, and everywhere the name of Robin Hood and his merry men was spoken with fond pride by the common people.

In his way he was considered as irreproachable as King Arthur himself, for in some ways the laws of the merry men were as ideal as those of the Round Table. No sick, or poor, or unfortunate ever appealed to Robin Hood in vain, and it would have been considered a disgrace to the band to have made war upon women or children. And so good was the reputation of the band in this respect that Robin Hood was looked upon as the knight errant of the people, bound to succor the distressed, battle for the right, and relieve all women in trouble. It is true that he robbed the rich, but he said expressly that he did it in order to give alms to the poor, and no one was so ready as he to imperil his life for the innocent or afflicted. It was also believed by the people that he was truly religious, and followed the life of a highwayman from a sense of duty, and as a protest against the unjust laws of the land. Indeed, one of the favorite anecdotes in regard to him is that which relates how, on one occasion, the officers of the king coming suddenly upon him while his band was celebrating mass, he refused to stir out of reverence for the sacrament, but waited for the priest to conclude the ceremony, and then falling upon the officers with great zeal, utterly routed them, giving the ransoms and spoils which he obtained to the church as a thank offering.

Thus lived Robin Hood and the merry men who looked upon Sherwood Forest as their rightful home, and from the first hour of the day, when they would be up and away to the hunt, their green coats indistinguishable from the glistening forest leaves, and their horns leading the foresters a merry dance through the thicket, to the time of retiring when they lay down on their leafy couches, they kept good consciences, feeling that they had spent the day well if by chance they had had the luck to rob a wealthy merchant, or a pompous abbot, or an officer in the king's livery. Whenever a particularly interesting encounter occurred, it

was repeated from village to village and shire
to shire, until the whole country was familiar
with it, and the village poet would straightway
put it in rhymes which would be sung everywhere.   Thus all the adventures of Robin
Hood came gradually to be sung by the people,
just as in the earlier times the bards sang the
songs of Taliesin ; and although these ballads
were not written down or collected for a long
time afterward, yet they represent the life of
those times so truly that they are more valuable
in that respect than the books which were then
being written in Latin, and which dealt with philosophy and religion.

And in the literature which followed this time
we see how deeply these ballads had impressed
the mind of the people—an impression which
lingers to this day in localities which claim to
hold some memento of the people's hero. Here
we find Robin Hood cairns, crosses, penny
stones, wells, chairs, and trees, Robin Hood's
bed, and his stable, and the chasm across which
he leaped ; while many of the popular games of
England are said to have originated in a desire

to perpetuate his memory. For centuries there was a special Robin Hood Day which was celebrated all over the country, and which was held in as great esteem as more important holidays. It occurred in May, and became in time a principal part of the spring festivals. On May Day, the youth would rise immediately after midnight and go to the adjoining woods, where they would cut fresh boughs, and adorn themselves with wreaths and flowers. At sunrise they would return home, hang garlands on the doors and windows of the houses, and then erect the May-pole which had been brought home by twenty yoke of oxen, each ox having nosegays of flowers tied on the tips of his horns, the May-pole itself being bound with wreaths of flowers from top to bottom and tied with banners, flags, and gay handkerchiefs at the top. After it was set up, the ground around was strewed with green boughs and flowers, and bowers and arbors were erected near. Then followed the dance, which was joined in by old and young, after which came feasting and merrymaking until night, when bonfires were lighted and all the company played games in honor of Robin Hood.

Later on Robin Hood and his men came to be the heroes of many plays and dramas, in which the great hero himself, Little John, Scarlett, and Friar Tuck lived again before the people and delighted their hearts, as they had delighted their ancestors in the days when the merry men were real personages. And a study of the literature of England for long afterward reveals the large place which the Sherwood Forest outlaws held in the popular heart. When the ballads were finally collected—probably about the last of the fifteenth century—it was found that, as far as their influence on literature was concerned, they had done their work centuries before, and that, like the stories of King Arthur, they were making the popular literature while yet unwritten, except in the hearts of the people.

CHAPTER VIII.

LANGLANDE—GOWER.

The Norman conquest exercised an influence over England for nearly two centuries and a half, during which time the country could not really be called English, as the laws, books, language, and religious instruction were all in French.   This period is often spoken of, therefore, as the Anglo-Norman period, showing that although the kings who reigned, and the nobility who flourished, were all French in their education, yet they, with the mass of the people, were English in many ways of thinking.   The fourth king after William the Conqueror had a Saxon mother, and this did more to reconcile the people to the reigning power than anything else could have done, though they yet suffered greatly from the tyranny of the upper classes.

During this time of change, when the country

was neither French nor English, and everything was in an unsettled state, we have seen that the people cared very little about books. And although there were learned men who wrote works in Latin about religion, philosophy, and other deep matters, yet the only literature which attracted the people was the popular legends of old British heroes, such as the story of King Arthur by Geoffrey of Monmouth, and as it was added to later on by other writers, the songs of Charlemagne and other French heroes whom the Normans loved, and above all the ballads and stories which related to the people's hero, Robin Hood; these last being so thoroughly English in the hatred which they show to the tyranny of the nobility, that they may be said to express the very voice of the people during the Norman supremacy. But this time of unrest and change came to an end at last, and left the Saxon race still ruler of England, for in spite of laws, religion, oppression, and injustice of every kind, the people would not become Norman. They would not speak French, they would not learn to read and write it, they would not tolerate French ways; if a Norman married a Saxon he had to learn her language, and their children spoke the mother's tongue, while the peasants would rather have their children wandering like outlaws through the forests than to see them attending French schools.

And so gradually the country became almost entirely English again, the French influence upon the mass of the people having been so slight that, though the upper classes retained many French characteristics, at the beginning of the fourteenth century the English peasant was very much the same as the Saxon peasant during the time of Alfred, being a stalwart, robust fellow, very fond of plenty to eat and drink, faithful to his friends, generous to his foes, and quite unable to understand how any foreigner should dare to look upon England as anything else than the country of the English.

This change became so universal that there was no more question as to the position of England among the other nations of Europe, and indeed, before fifty more years had passed away Western Europe was called upon to see

France itself defending its crown from an English sovereign who professed to have a claim on it through his mother, Isabella, daughter of Philip II. This was Edward III., tenth king from the Conqueror, whose greatest boast was that he was an Englishman, and whose reign is signalized as one of the most important in English history.

Edward III. came to the throne when he was but fourteen years of age, and as he reigned for fifty years, the history of his reign is really the history of England for a half century of wonderful development. In the beginning of his reign French was still the language of the court, though it was hardly known among the common people, and his education had been in every respect that of a royal youth during the latter part of the Norman period. Society was still divided into classes consisting of the nobility, knights, tradesmen, and yeomen, and each class differed in its ideas of educating the young. The education of a gentleman was said to be complete when he could hold and use a spear gracefully and effectively, fence, hold a hawk on his wrist in the approved fashion, ride fearlessly, dance well, and carve cleanly ; while book learning was " left to louts."   Fine dressing among the knights and nobles was carried to the greatest extravagance.   Velvets, silks, and fine cloth, embroidered with seed pearls, gold, and silver, formed the mantles and robes, supplemented by fancy shoes and stockings, hats and bonnets ornamented often with feathers and precious stones, and in the case of the ladies elaborate hair-dressing, the hair being often twisted through with gold threads and jewels.   The castles were furnished with all the magnificence that the owner could afford, the great hall showing by the rests for armor, spear, and sword, and the perches for bird and hawk, what was considered the chief business in life.

The peasant wore leather breeches, a woollen frock, rough shoes of untanned hide, and was taught chiefly to be always ready at the call of his lord for service in war.   The practices of chivalry were still kept up throughout England, and during the reign of Edward III. it seemed as if the days of King Arthur and his knights had returned, for the English court became celebrated throughout Europe for its magnificence and chivalry. Even before the king's name had become formidable on account of his deeds in the French war, his court was thronged by adventurers and the oppressed of other nations who flocked to England to ask his support; and alliance with the English throne was courted by all the little kingdoms of Europe which feared the power of the great empires.

The love for pageants and display of all kinds was uncontrolled, and one festival only succeeded another. In one year Edward proclaimed fourteen tournaments, some of which lasted three weeks. Not satisfied with this, he proclaimed a Round Table, or great international tournament in honor of King Arthur, and gave orders for the building at Windsor of a house to be called the Round Tower, in which the knights should banquet. This tower had to be built in great haste, and messengers were sent all over England to impress workmen into the service. These men dug out stone, felled trees, prepared lime and sand-pits, and carried on the work with such a will, that soon the tower arose fair and strong, and it seemed to the people that their king had the gift of the magician and could do whatever he would. Then Edward sent all over Europe, inviting the free knights to come to the tournament, and they responded willingly, all but the knights of France, who could not come because their king forbade them. And the magnificence of this tournament—during which time the streets of London were strewed with sand daily to prevent the horses from slipping—raised the fame of Edward III. even higher than before, until it seemed that for glory and magnificence he could rank with Arthur himself.

Besides the love of great pageants and military displays, the English still kept a great fondness for the chase, and the royal hunting expeditions were very fine affairs. For days before the hunt bridges were repaired, paths opened, and all persons forbidden under a heavy fine to disturb the game ; while the court was all astir with excitement, for every detail was carefully attended to, great care being taken to sound the horns musically, while even the voices of the dogs were skilfully matched so that the cry of the whole pack would be melodious. And every event was in like manner made the occasion for as great display as possible. When Edward's bride, Philippa of Hainault, came to England to be married and crowned, every city through which she passed received her with great pageants, and when Edward visited France his interview with the French king was a gorgeous ceremonial, in which even the dressing played a great part, Edward wearing a robe of crimson velvet embroidered with golden leopards, a crown of jewels on his head, a jewelled sword, and gold spurs; while the French king wore a robe of blue velvet embroidered with fleurs-de-lis of gold, and all the courtiers and knights were likewise attired in great magnificence.

Yet, in spite of the splendor of the court, life in England at that time was very primitive in many ways. There was no postal system, although the king was general of an immense army, and if knight or noble wished to send a letter he was obliged to send a squire or page on horseback, even though the distance extended from one end of the kingdom to the other. And although velvet and silk and jewel were used in robing knight and lady, and in trappings for the horses, yet the floor of castle and hut alike was strewn with rushes; while, except for the blazing fires and the presence of a few wax tapers, the dwelling of the noble was as dark at night as the hovel of the peasant who went to bed by the light of the first stars.

Rich and poor alike rose at sunrise, and dined at nine o'clock in the morning, in the castle the family being summoned to the meal by the blowing of a horn. As each one entered the hall he was served with an ewer and towel for the washing of his hands. On the table there were no forks or plates, but between each two guests were placed large slices of bread upon which was placed the meat. As each course was finished the bread was thrown into the almsbasket for the poor. After the meal the minstrels were called in, and the company listened to songs, stories, puzzles, and games.

Supper came at five o'clock, soon after which it was considered bed-time.

In those days hospitality was considered one of the chief virtues, and every stranger who craved admittance at the castle was warmly welcomed, it being thought the greatest rudeness to inquire his name or business, or to pry into his affairs. As a traveller or wayfarer, he received courtesy and kindness according to his station, whether he were guest of master or servant, and if he chose he could go his way without revealing even his name.

Such was life in England during the time of Edward III. But this reign, which was distinguished for the magnificence of the court; for its thirty-three years war with France—a war signalized by some of the most brilliant military achievements in history—for the loyal defence made by the Scotch for their country, which Edward tried his whole life to conquer; for the growth of trade in England, so that manufacturing cities may be said to date from that time; and for the many excellent laws passed by the parliament in regard to the rights and needs of

9

the people, is also supremely celebrated as the birth-time of modern English literature.

Whatever may have been the influence of Norman thought upon the English mind, from this time forth the literature of all Englishmen was purely English, and although French and Latin were somewhat used by the writers who founded modern English, yet the spirit of the greatest work done then was English, and the writings of that period so firmly fixed the English language that it has changed very little since, excepting in outward form.

In England, the work of fixing the language in permanent form was not due to one writer alone—as in Italy, for example, Italian was measurably fixed by the great poet Dante—though it is sometimes considered that, among those who contributed to this result the poet Chaucer should have the greatest honor; but it seemed that the different classes into which society was divided was each to have a representative. Thus one man—Chaucer—spoke the voice of the court. Another—Wickliffe—represented the learned scholar of the day; and another—Langlande—was the people's voice, and answered back to Caedmon across the interval of eight centuries as clearly as if the antiphon had never been interrupted. These three men, together with two others of less importance, Gower and Mandeville, formed the great group of writers from whom modern English literature dates. Each had his own part to do, and each performed it well, as men conscious of the great task before them.

Of the poet Langlande, but little is known except that he was a poet, and gave to English literature, while still in its infancy, one of the greatest allegories in the language. He was a priest, and is said to have been the son of a free man ; but although this may have mattered at the time when to be the son of a free man meant certain important liberties, it matters little now, when the world knows Langlande only as a man who, amid the glittering magnificence of Edward's court saw still the poverty and misery of the people, the oppression of the rich and powerful, the dishonesty of a large part of the clergy, and all the dreadful ills which beset a nation which believes that men are born unequal, and that brotherhood is but a name.

Langlande's poem is called *The Vision of Piers Plowman*, and relates, under the form of a dream—a form allegorical writing was apt to take at that time—all the misery that England was then suffering, though if one looked only on the outside of things, as seen in the splendor of the court, it would appear a happy and prosperous time.

Langlande tells us that as he was wandering, one May morning, on Malvern Hills, he grew weary and lay down in the grass to rest himself with sleep. And while he slept there came to him a vision of a fair meadow, to the east of which was a height on which stood a tower, and to the west a valley full of mists and shadows. And the meadow was full of people of all kinds, rich and poor, high and low, priests, beggars, palmers, minstrels, pilgrims, tradesmen, farmers, friars, waifs, and strays, who all went wandering through the meadow pursuing their several callings, as was the manner of men in life. And the poet perceived from this that the meadow represented the world, and that all these people were men and women come in the likeness of a dream. And from the castle on the height there came to him a fair lady and said--" Why sleepest thou ? " And he was afraid of her, although she was so beautiful, but yet he gathered courage and asked her what the vision meant; and she told him that the tower on the hill was the abode of Truth, which would lead man into all good ways ; and that the dark vale held the castle of Care, where Falsehood dwelt ; and that the meadow signified the world ; and that all who did well and lived nobly should after death go eastward to abide forever in heaven, where Truth was enthroned ; and that all who did ill and lived wickedly should at the end of their lives go westward, and dwell forever in the valley of mist and shadow.

Then he knelt on the ground and asked her to show him how he should know Truth from Falsehood, and she told him to look on his left hand and there he would see Falsehood, who was in appearance a beautiful woman richly clothed, wearing a crown on her head, and wearing rings set with rubies and other precious stones—which meant that he that does wrong may in this life meet with great honor, but still he will come at last to the vale of darkness. And then the fair lady left him, telling him to find out the meaning of the rest of the vision for himself. And then the dreamer saw that every man and woman in the meadow represented some vice or fault by whose name they were called. If a man were proud of his station, he was called Pride ; if envious, he was called Envy ; if fond of money, Avarice, and so on ; and in his dream Langlande saw all the things that they did, and knew that the vision was true ; for as these people acted in the meadow, so did the people act in the world, where the rich oppressed the poor, and the strong took advantage of the weak.

But after a while some of these people grew tired of their way of living, and went to a palmer and asked him whence he came. And he told them he came from the East, and had visited Alexandria, Damascus, Babylon, Bethlehem, and Sinai. Then they asked him if he had ever been to the dwelling place of a saint called Truth, for they had heard of him and wished to find him. But the palmer answered that he had never heard of this saint, and never before had met anyone who inquired of him. But at this, a plowman who stood by spoke up, and said that he had known Truth for forty years, and that he would gladly show them the way to his dwelling. This plowman was the Piers after whom the poem is named, and his humble station in life showed that he who did his duty bravely and truly could be the friend of Truth, no matter how lowly his lot. Then Piers told the company that whoever would reach the dwelling of Truth must choose death rather than commit any sin, and at all times do unto others as they would have others do to themselves, love their enemies, and give alms to the poor; for he who did not these things could never keep in the path that led to the castle of Truth, but would lose his way continually, because the nature of the ground was such that all who committed sin would straightway lose their reckoning and not know whether to turn to the right or the left, to turn back or go ahead; while he who did right would see the path ever before him, and come at last to the place of his desires.

Then the poem relates all the adventures and misfortunes of the people in the meadow, introducing all the evils that England was then suffering from—the selfishness of the rich, the poverty of the poor, the ceaseless wars, the heavy taxes, the covetousness of the clergy, the famine caused by the failure of crops, and the great pestilence called the Black Death, which had just swept over England and destroyed in some places half the population. All these evils were introduced into this wonderful allegory with a skill so marvellous that the poem has a priceless value, as showing the condition of society at that time, and is considered the best picture of that period that can be obtained.

Piers Plowman was popularly supposed to typify some exalted hero or saint, whose pure life should be an example to others, and thus lead them to better things. This is what the hero meant to those who read the book when it was first written, though it is evident that Langlande himself saw in Piers Plowman only the yearning for the noble and good which still remained in the English people, and strove to make it plain that, only by following this impulse for the right, could a purer national life be reached. The poem is remarkable for its form, which is like that of the old Saxon poems written before the Conquest, when rhymes were not used, and alliteration distinguished poetry from prose. Thus it shows, as no other work had done, how little the common people had been affected by the Norman influence; for Langlande wrote entirely for the people, and appealed to them in the way that would soonest reach them. In using the language of the masses, in introducing again the old metres, and in the deep seriousness of his subject, Langlande departed entirely from the French ideas of poetry, which demanded musical words, easy rhymes, and subjects that would amuse the hearers, who wanted only to hear of romance and gay adventures. Thus Piers Plowman was really a Saxon poem, and pleased the English heart which loved to be stirred by deep emotions and serious thoughts; for that was natural to the race which loved fighting, and conquest, and glory better than anything else, and which laid the foundations of England's greatness in its love of justice and respect for duty, even while it was yet heathen, and knew of no better lot than continual fighting both in this life and after death.

Thus it is by the character of his poem that Langlande connects English literature with Beowulf and Caedmon; and at the same time his was one of the first voices to speak the evil that was flourishing in the state and church, and to point out the necessity for reform. That the poem reached the heart of the common people is shown by its immense popularity with the nation at large, and by the fact that many succeeding writers tried to gain a hearing for their works by producing works similar to *Piers Plowman*.

Nothing can better show the great change made in the English language and literature during the fourteenth century than the works of John Gower, whose first important book was written in Norman French, because that language was yet spoken at court, and whose last, written toward the close of a long life, was in the English of the period.

The first of these books, called *Speculum Meditantis—The Mirror of Thought*—was devoted to a description of the vices and virtues of the age, and pointed out the way by which wrong-doers might return to the path of duty. This book was widely read by those familiar with its language, that is, by the upper classes, but it made no lasting impression, and was not as fine in a literary sense as some French ballads of Gower, which showed him at his best as a poet. The *Speculum Meditantis* is now entirely lost, and the only importance attached either to it or the ballads lies in the fact that Gower was the last poet of any consequence who wrote in French. Another work in Latin (the scholar's language), called the *Vox Cla-*

mantis—The Voice of One Crying, is much more valuable, as it shows the bitter feeling which then existed between the common people and the higher classes. If other historical evidence were wanting this book would be invaluable, as showing the condition of England at that time.

His last book, written in English (the popular language), although it had a Latin title, was called *Confessio Amantis—The Confession of a Lover*, and consists of a number of stories of romance, the whole book being not unlike the collections of tales for which the French and Italian writers were famous. It was written, indeed, at the request of the king for something for his own reading. So that its use of the English language for court literature is really a very notable event, which marks an important date in the history of English literature.

All of Gower's works show that he was a man of immense learning, and that he felt the stir of the times; but he had not the genius to give the real feeling of the day a voice, and so his writings made no impression upon the people at large, though he was popular with writers and thinkers, and those to whom literature meant the setting of a love-tale to smooth and easy rhymes. His chief importance rests on the fact that he was among the first to recognize and make use of the newly-formed English language, and give it a place in the literature which attracted the upper classes.

CHAPTER IX.

SIR JOHN MANDEVILLE.

As we have seen, the books most popular with the English people after the Norman invasion were principally written in poetry, and the stories of adventure and tales of bravery, which the nation chiefly delighted in, were all in the form of songs or ballads, or the long poems called metrical romances, whose length prevented them from being sung, and which were written in Latin and French as well as in English. But during this period, when the people cared more about being amused than being instructed, there was one book, written in prose, which the nation at large found so delightful and fascinating that it may be said to have been the chief means of creating an interest in something outside of poetry, and by some it is considered to

be the real beginning of English prose literature.

This book, which so affected the national
taste, was written by Sir John Mandeville, and
was a history of his travels and adventures in
various parts of the world. Mandeville was
born in the year 1300, nearly two hundred
years before the discovery of America, and at
a time when the ignorance of Western Europe
about the rest of the world was something
amazing. A great traveller was such a curiosity in those days that his name was known
equally well in France, Spain, Germany, Italy,
or England, no matter in which of these countries he had been born, and the most incredible stories he could tell were eagerly believed
by the readers of his book. This was owing
partly to the fact that people were really anxious to learn all that they could of foreign
countries, and partly to the love of the marvellous, which is found to be greatest always
where there is least knowledge.

The first reason accounted for the honor in
which all travellers were held and the respect

that was shown them, and made kings and princes become their willing entertainers; while their journey from one court to another, after their return from a foreign tour, was almost like a triumphal procession. And thus it happened that a traveller could very easily deceive his listeners or hearers, for in their eagerness to be instructed they received everything that he said as truth. Indeed, it would have been a hard matter to have done otherwise, as travelling was a pleasure indulged in by few, and no matter how incredible the story told by the traveller, he was almost always sure that there would be found no one with sufficient knowledge or experience to gainsay it.

The crusades had widened men's minds in regard to certain portions of the world, and Western Europe had ceased to think that Arabs and Turks were monsters, only half human, and in league with supernatural powers. But this only seemed all the more reason to suppose that there were in other parts of the world just such creatures as they had once believed the Arabs and Turks to be, for the love

of the marvellous dies hard, and it was easier
to believe that there were races with two
heads and one eye living somewhere, than to
believe that the traveller who had first reported their existence should have been de-
ceived himself, or capable of deceiving his
listeners.

To travel in those days required the same
leisure and wealth that had been necessary four
hundred years before, in Alfred's time, when
only the most adventurous spirits ever left their
native land, for the conditions were almost exactly the same. Men still traversed the sea in
slow-sailing vessels, and travelled on foot or by
horse all over every land that was not desert.
It was still as necessary to be provided with a
band of courageous followers to protect the
traveller as in the days when Wulfstan and
Othere related their adventures to Alfred's court.
And the East, that region of the marvellous,
where all impossibilities seemed possible, was
just as much a source of wonder as it had been
before the crusades had shown that man is
everywhere very much the same, and that a

Mohammedan was as capable of serving truth, honor, and justice as the Christian foe who came to oppose him.

And so, when Mandeville was born at St. Albans, the world as known to England was still a very curious place. The western continent was unknown, and undreamed of; Eastern Asia, though known to exist, was regarded almost as the fancy of adventurous travellers, and the Atlantic Ocean was supposed to reach from Western Europe to the outermost edge of the earth, which was thought to be flat and to be peopled with monsters and demons. St. Albans, known in the history of the Church as the place where the first Christian martyr met his death, was an unimportant place, and it is almost impossible to find any records of importance relating to Mandeville's early years. The few books that tell anything of his childhood relate that from his earliest years he showed a great fondness for study, and that he was " ravished with a mightie desire to see Asia and Africa." This wish, he says himself, came to him first when as a child he listened to the stories told

by one who had travelled all over the world.
Perhaps, too, the condition of the country at that
time had some influence upon the boy, for the
spirit of the crusades was still strong in men's
minds, and only a little more than twenty years
before Mandeville's birth, Edward I., the pride
of England, had won golden laurels in fighting
with the Turk.

And while Mandeville was studying hard at
theology, philosophy, medicine, and natural
science, he must also have spent many an hour
in poring over the romantic stories which were
then so popular, and in which knight, lady, and
esquire played such an important part; he must
also have listened to the tales of crusaders
returned from the Holy Land. Strange stories
had they to tell of Saracen and Turk, of the
great battles fought around the walls of Jerusalem, of the brave deeds of knight, and soldier,
and page under the banner of the crimson cross,
and of the equally brave deeds of Moslem chieftain and serf under the banner of the silver
crescent ; of the beautiful mosques and temples
where the pagans worshipped, and which were

considered too holy for a Christian to enter; and of the land itself, with its fair skies stretching over forest and stream, and hills and meadows, forever sacred to the crusaders because they had known the presence of the Master in whose service they fought.

And it is not strange that the impressions received during his childhood should have been of such a lasting character as to affect Mandeville's whole life, for the times in which he lived were full of the unrest which war always brings, and to a child listening to the talk of his elders, it could only seem that peaceful staying at home was but a part for women and children, and that the sphere of true manhood was on the field fighting gloriously, or following adventures which only brave and knightly hearts could take pleasure in. When he was about twenty-two years of age, Mandeville left England, and was absent over thirty years travelling in the East, and it was after his return home that he wrote the book which made his name so famous. Still influenced by the supreme place which the Holy Land had always occupied in the English mind since the beginning of the crusades, he called his book *The Way to Jerusalem*, adding that it also treated of the marvels of India, with many other strange isles and countries.

Strange indeed were the wonders related in this old book of Tartary, Persia, Ethiopia, Egypt, India, China, and the Holy Land, called by the author the "most worthy and excellent land, the lady and sovereign of all others, and passing all in beauty and promise." Here were accounts of great rivers, fed by mountain streams, which rushed into the sea with such power and speed that the waters were fresh twenty miles out from land. And of mountains which passed the clouds, and whose shadows stretched three score miles away, while the air above them was so clear that no wind ever blew over them, and letters traced by the fingers in the dust of the rocks would be found there a year afterward untouched by rain or breath of wind. And there is also an account of some of the marvels that were seen, such as a pit of shining gravel of which beautiful vessels of glass were made, and which always remained full, no matter how much was taken away from it, because it was supposed to be an outlet of a sea of gravel which rose and fell with the tides.

And then he relates all the marvels that he saw in the Holy Land, and all the historic places that he visited. He tells of the tree which dropped its leaves at the time of the Crucifixion, and which was never to be green again, until Jerusalem was taken from the infidels; and of a convent where the monks kept plenteous supply of olive-oil, which was made entirely from the olives which the birds brought there every year as offerings ; and of tombs of saints, altars, relics, and other things of interest to his readers, who were all devout believers in the traditions that had been gathering for centuries around the Holy Land.

But it was outside of the Holy Land that the greatest marvels were seen. And we have descriptions of gardens in Egypt having some trees which bore seven kinds of fruits, and others which bore a fruit called apples of Paradise, because no matter into how many parts

the apple was divided, each piece would always
have in its centre the figure of the holy cross.
And in Ethiopia there were wonders also—men
with only one foot, which was so large that they
could shade themselves from the sun in the
heat of the day by using it as an umbrella, and
tribes that were of different colors at different
ages, and rivers full of great emeralds, and
monsters and other strange sights calculated to
delight the hearts of his readers.

Then there are stories of India and the
islands of the sea, and we hear of mines of diamonds and sapphires and other precious stones,
and of the strange people of every color, and of
the idols which they worshipped, and of the
forests and their fruits, and of wells whose water
would cure the sick and prevent future trouble,
and other marvels equally fascinating. But it
was of Cathay or China that Mandeville chiefly
delighted to talk, for here he stayed over a
year with his fellow-travellers at the court of
the great Khan. And he describes with
delight the greatness of the country, and its
beautiful cities which were visited constantly by

merchants from every part of the earth, who came to buy the spices and jewels and silks which were the products of this wealthy land. And we are told the number of the great cities, and the size of their walls and palaces, and how they were all connected by fine roads, and how the king's messengers passed from one city to another constantly, so that news was carried to all parts of the kingdom regularly and effic- iently, the couriers being entertained along the way at certain houses owned by the king and set apart for that purpose.

Mandeville related that the court of the great Khan was the most magnificent in the world, and gave a full description of it in his book. The capital of the empire possessed the most wonderful palace that had ever been known, the walls of which were two miles in extent, and the gardens so large that within them was a great hill on which was built another palace; while all about the hill and palaces were trees bearing all kinds of fruits, vines, hanging full of grapes, lakes wherein swam white swans and ducks with beautiful plumage, streams bordered

with trees and flowers and crossed by ornamental bridges, birds of wonderful beauty and
with voices of exquisite sweetness, and in fact
everything that could gratify the taste. A part
of the garden was set aside for a menagerie, and
here were gathered wild beasts from every part
of the globe, the enclosure being so arranged
that when the king wished he could witness the
combats to which the beasts were trained without leaving his window.

The hall of the great palace was of unusual
magnificence, the roof being supported by
twenty-four pillars of fine gold, and the walls
covered with the skins of beasts dyed blood-
red, and so highly polished that Mandeville
gravely declared that when the sun was shining
a man could scarcely look upon them. In the
centre of the palace was the king's seat, wrought
of gold and precious stones, the four corners
having four serpents of gold twined around them,
and the whole covered with silken nets strung
with great pearls. At the end of the great hall,
which was also used as a dining-hall, was the
emperor's throne, made of precious stones, bor-

dered with pure gold, studded with jewels, the steps leading up to it being also of gold and jewels. Lower down was the seat of the emperor's first wife, which was made of jasper and bordered with gold and precious stones; and still lower down the seats of the second and third wife, of the same costly materials, which were followed by the places of the great ladies of the land in the order of their rank; while on the opposite side sat the emperor's son next to the throne, and beneath him the great lords of the realm in succession. And before each seat was placed a table, the emperor's being of gold and jewels and crystal, and the others decorated in like manner. All around the tables and the throne, and along the walls, twined a vine made of fine gold having clusters of white, red, black, green, and yellow grapes hanging from it, the fruit being made of crystal, rubies, onyx, beryl, emeralds, and topazes, and the imitation so perfect that Mandeville declared that it seemed a true vine bearing real fruit.

All the vessels which were used at table were of fine gold studded with precious stones, the drinking-cups being of emerald, or topaz, or sapphire; and during the feasts the king's magicians would bring in great tables of gold on which were placed peacocks and doves, and other birds, made of gold nicely enamelled, and these were made to dance, and clap their wings, and perform various tricks; for the magicians of Cathay were the most wonderful in the world, and knew of tricks and juggleries that were quite unknown to other nations. Under the emperor's table sat four clerks whose business it was to take down every word that was said, whether it were good or evil, for it was the law of the land that the king might never change or revoke any word that he ever said; and before the throne stood the great lords and barons, who served him and might never speak until the king gave them permission; for all had to keep silence, except the minstrels and players who were appointed to amuse the court while at table.

The dresses of the lords and ladies were in keeping with the rest, and were so costly that Mandeville said that if a man in England had but one robe such as those worn by the great nobles of Cathay, he would never be poor again. Four thousand nobles were chosen as governors of the great feasts, and these were divided into companies of four, each company being dressed in a different color. One had robes of cloth of gold and green silk, wrought with precious stones; the second company were dressed in red silk broidered with gold and pearls; the third were robed in purple, and the fourth in yellow, all glittering with jewels, and these nobles proclaimed the opening of the feast by passing before the emperor two and two, being followed by the minstrels with music and songs.

And in order to show the respect that was paid to learning in that country, all the great scholars and philosophers were given places of honor at the feast, and each one sat before a golden table on which were placed the instruments of his profession. Before some would be vessels of gold full of burning coals, before others vessels of crystal filled with water and wine and oil, before others golden spheres, astrological instruments, crucibles, time-pieces, and every kind of instrument showing the advance and the wonders of science.

And then there were keepers of wild beasts who brought in lions, and leopards, eagles, vultures, fishes, and serpents, who were trained to do reverence to the emperor. And these were followed again by more enchanters and jugglers, who did great marvels, making the sun and moon to shine, and then to fade away, so that it was day or night as they pleased; and then there was jousting and hunting of boars and deer, and hounds running through wild forests, all brought before the people's eyes by enchantment; and there was dancing, and feasting, and merriment until the feast was over, when all returned home singing the praises of the great khan whose riches and fame and generosity were beyond those of any other sovereign.

During the time that Mandeville passed there he travelled all through this famous country, and saw everything that it was possible to see; for he was a favorite with the Khan, who delighted to do him honor. After this he travelled

to other lands and saw many strange sights,
particularly in the realm of Prester John, a
mysterious personage who was much talked
of in those days, and who was supposed to rule
over a Christian community in the midst of
heathen lands, and who, when he went into battle, had no banners borne before him, but only
three crosses made of gold and precious stones ;
and when he rode on messages of peace he
had borne before him a platter of gold full
of earth to typify that great kings must turn at
last to dust, and another vessel full of gold and
jewels to signify his might ; for he was proud of
his great kingdom and fought as bravely as any
heathen to defend it in war.   And the gates of
his palace were of sardonyx, and the great
tower had two great disks of gold whereon
blazed two carbuncles of such size and brilliance
that they shone out on the night like crimson
stars.   And the tables off which he ate were of
emerald and amethyst and gold, and the steps
leading to his throne were of onyx and jasper
and sardonyx and cornelian, and the footstool
was of crystal bordered with fine gold and pre-

cious stones. In fact Prester John was almost as magnificent a sovereign as the great Khan himself, though he bore before him in all his journeys a little unpainted cross, to show his humility and meekness.

And so Mandeville travelled from one place to another, coming to Rome at last to do honor to the Pope and receive absolution for all the sins he had been obliged to commit while wandering in strange lands. And when he got back to England he knew of nothing more worthy than to sit down and write over the history of his travels, the book being received with such favor that, although it is supposed that the first copy was in Latin, it was speedily translated into French, English, German, Italian, Flemish, and other languages, and was considered the most interesting book in prose that had ever been written for the people. The wonders that were related in this book were not all unfamiliar to the people of Western Europe, but this perhaps only added to its value, for it was delightful to be assured by such a great traveller that there were countries inhabited by griffons and dragons ; and mountains which sent out rivers full of precious stones ; and places where trees would begin to grow from the seed at sunrise, bear fruit at midday, and sink back into the earth again at night ; and of a sea of crystal which rose and fell with tides, and on which no craft might pass to discern the land on the other side ; and many other marvels too numerous to record.   Perhaps not the least wonder was the fact that the people of these strange lands had letters and books unlike those of the Europeans, for more than once Sir John writes down the alphabets of these languages in order that his readers may compare them with their own.

Many doubts have been held as to whether Mandeville really did travel all over the countries that he pretended to have visited, and some scholars claim that his book was merely a compilation of other books of travel, and that there was perhaps no such person as Sir John Mandeville, and that his travels only existed in the imagination of some other writer.   But however that may be, the fact remains the same, that a book known as the travels of Sir John Mandeville did make its appearance in England at this time, that it was received by various nations as the authentic records of an English traveller, and that as a book it made a deep impression upon the minds of the people, and first gave to English prose a charm that it had not possessed before. That the author, following the custom of other travellers, should people the places he did not visit with monsters and dragons, and give ear to many idle tales in regard to other wonders, added, of course, to its fascination in a credulous age.

CHAPTER X.

The greatest writer of the fourteenth century, and one of the noblest poets in English literature, was Geoffrey Chaucer, who was born in 1328, one year after Edward III. came to the throne.

Very little is known of his life, and although London is supposed to have been the place of his birth, even that has been doubted; but the little that we do know tells us that he was probably a page at the court, and thus became early familiar with all the gorgeous ceremonials that distinguished the English court at that time. We also know that he was made a knight, that he fought in the French wars, was made a prisoner in France, held a place in the government, and married a maid of honor, whose sister was afterward the wife of one of the king's sons.

Thus there is no question about his position in society, and we must suppose from this that his family was one of importance, as it was not usual for any but the sons of gentlemen to be admitted as pages at court, and to the society of the nobility. His works show that he had the best education which the day could give, and that he was not only familiar with all the literature of the time, but had also studied mathematics, logic, philosophy, divinity, and perhaps some magic. Besides this, he must also have passed well in those branches which were the pride of the court, namely fencing, horsemanship, the use of arms, and all knightly accomplishments.

We can easily picture him as a boy, listening to the talk of those adventurous spirits which surrounded Edward III., and whose chief conversation would be of their own heroic deeds; for in those days there was not a little boasting, and the free lances, who loved to linger at the English court, were never backward in sounding their own praises. These free knights were men who had usually seen service in every country of Europe, and their talk was always of war and the glory of it, for they loved nothing else. And particularly while at the English court, they loved England, and desired to see her triumph over all her enemies. Their stories of adventures in German towns and Flemish cities, on highway and in castle, on coast and at sea, must have held a strange fascination for young Chaucer.

Then there were tales of the Scotch, who had dared to claim that Scotland should be free of England, and whose brave deeds in defence of their country were familiar in every English home, very few of which could not point to some chair left vacant since Edward's army had met defeat, and his generals had learned what sort of men were bred on Scottish moors and hills. And above all, there was talk of the French wars, and prophesies of England's greatness when her king should wear the crown of France, and of the promise of the king's son, afterward known as the Black Prince, the most daring knight in England, who was about Chaucer's age, and must have been regarded by the future poet as a worthy pattern for every loyal English boy. And in the intervals of fighting there were the grand tournaments, where knights jousted and ladies smiled on the winners, and jewels sparkled, and the whole scene was like a dream of fairy land, and one could scarcely believe that he was in England, whose people were suffering from hunger and disease and injustice; though of this Chaucer knew nothing then, as he had not yet received the poet's gift of seeing the bond which unites all men in brotherhood.

To a mind easily impressed, such as that of the young page, England in Chaucer's youth must have seemed the home of every virtue, for to be successful in arms, learned in chivalry, and accomplished in the graces of knighthood was considered the greatest thing in the world, and the English court and its circle of knights represented the very grace and flower of chivalry. Thus Chaucer had the advantage of seeing this side of life in its most glowing colors, and saw knighthood crowned and glorified; and this was an advantage he did not fail to make good

use of when he began his work as a poet, later
on.

And apart from these things, there were
others which must have made a lasting impression upon his young mind, for being well born
and well educated, he could command, and had
a taste for, the pleasures of a realm too often
neglected by his companions—the realm of literature ; and in the chronicles of Geoffrey of
Monmouth, the ballads of Robin Hood, and the
old war-chants of the Saxons, he must have
learned many a lesson of what life had meant
in those days when the English nation was
being built.   And so life must have seemed to
him very much like a succession of pictures,
some sad, some inspiring, and some gay; and
long before he reached manhood he must have
realized something of the meaning which lay
beneath the scenes, and wondered why one picture was so gloomy and another so full of brightness.

If it had been known from the beginning that
Chaucer was to be the greatest poet that England had produced up to that time, and that his

greatness was to consist, not so much in his rich imagination and fine fancy, which are indeed great, but in his knowledge of human nature and the portrayal of it, there could not have been a better education given him to fit him for his office than that which he received ; and his poems are as true pictures of the times as if the scenes he represented had been painted on canvas. To one, therefore, who wishes to know what England was during the fourteenth century, Chaucer is a true guide ; while his genius as a poet will make his works prized for their literary value as long as the English language endures.

When Chaucer first began to write, his poetry, as was natural, showed the influence of the impressions he had received in his youth, and he chose for his themes subjects familiar to the writers of the Anglo-French period, differing in this from his great predecessor, Caedmon, and his contemporary, Langlande. Among these earlier writings *The Romance of the Rose* is considered the most important. It was a translation of a part of a poem by that name which was famous all over Europe, and which every poet, minstrel, and courtier quoted continually. It was an allegory, written under the form of a dream, in which the hero starts out on an adventure having for its object the gathering of an enchanted rose, and relates how he was aided by some, and hindered by others, in his search for the magic flower. Those who aided him are persons who represent nobility and goodness, and those who hindered stand for the evils of the day, such as the poverty of the people, the dishonesty of the clergy, and so on.

But although this poem, and others of the same kind, made Chaucer instantly popular as a poet, they would have given him no lasting fame, and it is to a series of poems quite different in character that he owes his reputation. Familiar in his youth with the life of the court, military glory, and the delights of the student, he came also to know England in other ways ere he had grown old. And as his first knowledge of life had been like a series of brilliant pictures in which all seemed sunlight and glory, and flash of jewels, and ladies' smiles, so afterward he found himself looking on other pictures, in which he saw hungry faces of little children, wretched men and women living in filthy poverty, well-fed priests taking money from the hands of the poor, and the rich and strong taking advantage of the weak and suffering.

All these things made a deeper impression upon his heart than the splendid pageantries of Edward's court, and the serious work of his life was to portray England and English manners as seen in the nation at large, and to teach, if possible, some lesson that all might learn and profit by. And so his great work of all shows the true feeling he had, for he wrote it seriously and from his heart, thinking only of the work itself, and not whether it would please the knights and ladies of the court. And being a true poet, he put into it so much grace and beauty and noble thought that it could not help but endure, just as the work of any poet or painter or sculptor must endure if it be perfect and beautiful of its kind.

This work is called *The Canterbury Tales*, because the stories are supposed to be told by a number of pilgrims on their way to visit the shrine of Thomas à Becket, archbishop of Canterbury, who had been murdered and buried there nearly two hundred years before. Becket was considered a saint in the English church, and it was customary for pious persons to make pilgrimages to his shrine, either as penance for some sin, or to ask some favor, or to please their consciences with good works ; and as these pilgrimages were made from all parts of the kingdom, it happened that many strangers met together on the road ; and as every station in life held some who delighted in pilgrimages, it also happened that all sorts of people came together as the way approached Canterbury.

Chaucer's pilgrims came from all over the country, and from all classes, and represented high and low, rich and poor, all being equal for the time, as all were engaged in the same pious work. It was natural for these pilgrims to journey in companies, as the land was in an unsettled state always and the highways were dangerous to all travellers, who were at the mercy of any thieves or highwaymen who should choose to molest them. Great preparations were made for these pilgrimages, and as they were considered acts of great piety, the pilgrims always took advantage of any chance for amusement or entertainment that the journey afforded, feeling sure that their pious intentions entitled them to all the good cheer they could find.

Chaucer's pilgrims were all of this class. They were going to Canterbury on a very praiseworthy errand, and in the meantime they would make the journey as pleasant as possible. One of the favorite means of entertainment in all classes at that time was the telling of stories, and Chaucer has his twenty-nine pilgrims all agree to tell each a tale or more as they ride to Canterbury and return ; and it was decided that he who should tell the best story should be given a grand supper when the pilgrimage was over. The twenty-nine pilgrims had met at a certain inn, where Chaucer was stopping—for in the story he supposes himself also to be on a pilgrimage to Canterbury—and the host of the inn decides to join the company as they proceed, and to be the judge as to which story is the best.

Among the pilgrims is a Knight, who had fought in the East among the Saracens, and was therefore held in great honor, having been in fifteen battles, and fought thrice in single combat for the glory of Christianity, and whose sober dress and grave demeanor gave an air of great distinction to the party. With him was his son, a young Squire, with curled locks and fresh complexion, who wore a costume so gay that Chaucer said that his cloak, with its embroidered flowers of white and red, looked like a fair meadow; and the youth's spirits were so gay also that he went singing and playing on the flute all the day, being able to make songs as well as sing them. With these two was a Yeoman, an attendant, dressed in coat and cap of green, like one of Robin Hood's own men, bearing with him a mighty bow of ash, and having his sheaf well filled with arrows, tipped with peacock feathers for more gaudiness; wearing also sword and buckler, dagger and horn, and having his cropped head—which Chaucer says was as round as a nut and as brown—stuffed full of woodcraft, so that he must have been a valuable travelling companion, being able to tell by signs infallible the presence or absence of foes in the shadowy wood-paths, and knowing by the pressed grass or broken spider-webs, that the deer had been before them in their journey, and brushed the dew from the flowers; and scenting in the wind and in the curled leaves of the trees the promise of rain.

Then there was a gentle Nun, Madame Eglentine, whose voice sounded divinely sweet as she sang the service, and whose manners at table were a marvel to all beholders, being of such elegance that few could hope to imitate them. She also spoke French well, and took great delight in being courteous to all men, while her heart was so tender that she would weep at the sight of a dead mouse. She was fair to look upon, too, having a beautifully shaped nose of very aristocratic outline, and a small mouth, and eyes as gray as glass. And she wore fine, dainty clothing, and a brooch on which was engraved the legend—*Amor vincit omnia*—Love conquers all things—to show her kindness and great tenderness of heart.

Next came an Abbot who loved hunting above all things, and to whom the sound of the bells jingling on the bridle of his horse was better than the chapel bell ringing to prayers, and whose fine horses and fleet grayhounds made him the envy of all other abbots who also loved hunting. He was dressed as finely as an abbot need be, with his cloak trimmed with fur, and his hood fastened under his chin with a pin of gold curiously wrought; and altogether he was just such an abbot as Robin Hood would have liked to meet in Sherwood Forest, and compel to give up his fine cloak and his fine horse and the bagful of money that he loved.

Then there was a Clerk, or scholar of Oxford, noted for his love of learning, and preferring books to fine clothes or music, or anything that money could buy, borrowing from all his friends in order to get the precious volumes, and spending days and nights in reading them. And there was a Parson, and a Plowman, and a Miller, and a Weaver, and a Carpenter, and a Dyer, a Merchant, a Lawyer, a Sailor, a Doctor—and in fact all callings were represented in this company of pilgrims, for only in this way could there be a variety in the stories. And having rested at the inn over night, they started off gayly in the morning, for it was in the spring of the year, and the air was soft and sweet with the perfume of blossoms and early flowers, and the birds were singing, and all hearts were merry and glad. The descriptions of these characters all occur in the prologue to the stories, and are of great interest as true pictures of each class at that time.

The first one to tell a tale was the Knight, and, as was natural for so great a traveller, he did not speak of London, or France, or Italy, which places might have been familiar to some of the company; but his story was all about the East, and his heroes and heroines lived in Athens, that wonderful city which seemed like a dream to common folk; and in this way the good Knight was able to make his listeners fully understand how wonderful it was to be a great traveller. And this was his story:

Two young knights, named Arcite and Pala-mon, kinsmen and brothers in arms, were taken prisoners by the great Theseus, the conqueror of towns and people innumerable, and carried from Thebes, their home, captives to Athens. There they were placed in a tower to dwell in anguish and woe forever, for Theseus was so angry at the Thebans that he had sworn that no prisoner should ever be released either by pardon or ransom.   Now, Queen Hippolyta, whom Theseus had married after conquering her kingdom, had a sister, Emily, who had been brought to Athens with them, and who was fairer than the lily, sweeter than May flowers, and a rival in beauty of even the rose itself. And one May morning Emily rose up with the sun, and put on her finest dress, and braided her yellow hair, and went out in the garden to do homage to the month of May ; and as she walked through the garden she gathered flow-ers and made a garland for her head, singing all the while in a voice of such heavenly sweetness that it penetrated through the thick stone walls of the dungeon, and came to the ears of Palamon and Arcite.

And looking down through their barred window, they saw the beautiful Emily walking in the garden, and they both immediately fell in love with her, and had a fierce quarrel as to who should have her; and they certainly would have slain one another in jealousy, had they not remembered suddenly that they were both prisoners for life, and that they had no swords, and that they might as well be friends, as the fair Emily was not for either of them. But there came one day to Athens a friend of Theseus, who loved him better than anyone else in the world, and this friend Perithoüs was also a friend of Arcite; and for love of Perithoüs, Theseus let Arcite go without price or ransom, on condition only that if he were ever found in Athens again he should have his head cut off with a sword.

But Arcite cared nothing for his good fortune, being so full of love for Emily that he preferred his prison to his freedom, for there at least he had a chance to see her, and envied Palamon bitterly. And Palamon envied Arcite in return, and bewailed his fate that he was left in prison and could do nothing to win his lady love. And thus it went on for two years, when Arcite was suddenly advised in a dream to go to Athens in disguise, and try and win Emily for his own. So he came to Theseus's court and offered his service as a servant, and finally came to be page, and then squire, and was well liked by Theseus and all his knights. This went on for five years. And at the end of that time Palamon, by the help of a friend, broke his prison and escaped, and fled to a neighboring grove, intending to lie hidden there all day and in the night make his escape to Thebes.

But it happened, that very morning, that Arcite came out into the grove to gather a garland of woodbine and hawthorn, for it was again May, and he wished to wear a wreath in honor of the season. And he wandered up and down, singing happy songs to May; but suddenly his mood changed and he began to be sorrowful, for he thought of Emily, and how he was no nearer having her for his bride now than seven years before. Then he began sighing and speaking his grief aloud, and Palamon, who was watching him from behind a thick bush, knew him for the first time—for Arcite had changed so that his features had seemed quite strange—and came out of his hiding-place and fell to reproaching Arcite bitterly, and the two took up the quarrel where they had left it off, and only stopped long enough to agree to fight a duel the next morning. And when the hour came they fell to right heartily, and were in the midst of a brave piece of fighting, when who should come riding up but Theseus himself, with all his company of knights and ladies, Hippolyta and Emily among them, all clothed in green and merry of heart, for they were on a hunting expedition. And Theseus immediately rode in between the two combatants, and drawing his sword threatened, to cut off the head of the one who dealt the next blow.

Then Palamon spoke out recklessly, and told

Theseus that the squire whom he loved and trusted was no other than the faithless Arcite, and that he himself was Palamon, and that they were both fighting for the love of Emily the Fair. At which Theseus was so enraged that he threatened direful death to both, and only relented when Emily and all the ladies fell on their knees and besought him to be merciful. Then he yielded, and agreed that both Palamon and Arcite should come to his court a year from that time, each with a hundred knights, and that they should enter the lists, and whoso was victor should have Emily; and with this they parted.

And then Theseus built a noble theatre in which the combat was to take place, which was of such magnificence that it was celebrated all over the world; for every kind of craft was called in to decorate and make it beautiful. The theatre, which was unroofed, was a mile in circumference, with walls of stone, marble gates, and temples of Venus, Mars, Diana, and other divinities, wrought of marble and gold. The walls were decorated with beautiful paintings and carvings which represented events in history and mythology, the whole costing an immense sum, which Theseus paid willingly, as he desired the theatre to be as costly and magnificent as possible. And when the day of trial came the company which assembled was well worthy of such a place of reception, for the greatest kings and nobles and ladies came to see the lovers, whose history had become famous, and the beautiful Emily, who was the cause of such trouble between them. With Palamon came the king of Thebes, in a chariot of gold drawn by four white bulls, and followed by twenty white mastiffs, held with gold collars and leashes; and this king wore upon his head a crown of gold as thick as a man's arm, and studded with rubies and diamonds of priceless value. With Arcite came the king of Lydia, riding upon a bay steed which was covered with cloth of gold, and this king wore upon his head a crown of laurel leaves, and held upon his wrist a tame white eagle, while tame lions and leopards followed him around.

Theseus received his distinguished guests

with great honor, and there was feasting and great joy until the day of the combat. In the morning of that day Palamon arose early, while the lark was singing its first notes, and went to the temple of Venus, and promised to love and honor her above all other divinities, and to sacrifice on her altar wherever he should travel, if she would but grant him the victory. And the statue of Venus trembled as he spoke, and he took it for a favorable sign and went his way rejoicing. And Arcite went to the temple of Mars, and made a sacrifice on the altar, and promised life-long service if he had the victory; and the coat-of-mail on the statue began to ring, and a voice bade him be of good cheer, and he too went his way rejoicing.

And then there was great sound of preparation, polishing of shields and buckling of armor, and music of pipe and drum, trumpet and clarion; and at last all the company came to the theatre, and the heralds sounded the trumpets, and Palamon under the white banner of Venus, with his hundred brave knights, and Arcite under the red banner of Mars, with his hundred brave knights, advanced to the combat. And they fought fiercely and long, for Palamon's friends had sworn that he should be victor, and Arcite's friends had sworn that he should be victor, and the people cheered now one and now the other, being equally willing to see either side win. But finally Palamon was overborne and the victory was with Arcite, and the shouts went up to the skies; and Emily smiled upon Arcite sweetly, for it was not in her heart to refuse her favor to so brave a conqueror.

And all would have been over, had not Venus fallen to weeping and wailing because her knight was overthrown, and the sound of her lamentation filled all Olympus, and her tears fell in floods on the earth, till at length good old Saturn, who could not bear to see her suffer, bade her leave off crying, for she should have her will; and he sent a fury, which rose from the ground and frightened Arcite's horse, and the hero was thrown on the hard ground, and struck his head and received his death-blow; for though they carried him to the palace carefully and nursed him tenderly it did no good, and he died at last, blessing Emily and bidding her to wed Palamon. And Theseus made him a grand funeral, and all the lords and ladies threw jewels, and gold, and perfume, and wine, and honey, and milk, and incense, and wreaths of flowers upon the bier where Arcite lay, covered with a cloth of gold, with a garland of laurel on his head, and his sword in his hand, and Emily fired the funeral pyre with her own hand, as was the custom for the chief mourner, and the flames mounted higher and higher, and soon there was an end of brave Arcite. And after a proper time had passed, Palamon and Emily were married, and thus the Knight's Tale ended with the jingle of wedding-bells, which was what the pilgrims all liked to hear.

Then there were other stories, some grave, some gay, and the pilgrims discussed each as it was told, and compared it favorably or unfavorably with the others. Among them was the story told by the Clerk, or Oxford scholar, who sent his wits roving among all the learned books he had read, and finally selected a tale from an Italian poet, and put it into English dress and called it the Story of Griselda.

Griselda was the daughter of a poor peasant, and supported her father and herself by keeping sheep, gathering herbs, and doing other small offices. But so beautiful was she and so sweet in manner that every one who passed by was attracted to her and stood in admiration before her. The lord of the land, whose palace stood not far off, had often noticed the grace and beauty of the peasant maid, and he resolved to make her his wife. But he said nothing of this to her, as he wished to surprise her; but had beautiful clothes made, and bought gems and rare ornaments to deck his bride when he should claim her. The people of the land were rejoiced when he told them of his intention to marry, and the wedding-day was appointed, and the guests all assembled, and waited with great curiosity for the bride to appear. But the marquis had kept his choice a secret, and everybody supposed he had won some great lady for his bride.

Griselda hurried through with her tasks, and thought that she would go with her companions and stand by the way-side, and see the grand company pass by, and get a look at the bride who was coming to rule over the land. But as she came in the cottage door, bringing with her a pail of water from the well, she heard her name called and saw the marquis standing near, and she went and knelt down before him and asked him what was his will; and he said that he desired to speak with her father and her apart, and first obtaining the old peasant's consent he begged Griselda to be his wife, and she agreed, though wondering greatly that he should choose one so humble as herself. Then the ladies of the court arrayed her in the beautiful clothes that had been made for her, and she was wedded to the marquis, and every one said that for beauty and dignity she equalled the greatest lady in the land, and that the marquis had made a good choice.

And all went well until it came into the head of the marquis to try his wife's faith, and find out whether she loved him for himself alone or for the great position he had given her. So he began to treat her very cruelly; but Griselda did not complain, and said nothing even when he took her two children from her and sent them away, telling her that she had promised to obey him in all things and must not hinder him in this. Griselda even thought that both her children were slain, for they had been taken away by a man who was famous for his cruelty and savage temper. But though year after year went by while the marquis kept up his cruel treatment, Griselda was still patient under it all, because of the promise she had made to obey him in all things. And year after year the people loved her the more, and hated the marquis, whom they thought a wicked husband and the murderer of his children.

But the marquis had really sent the children out of the country to live with a relative, and be tenderly nurtured, as became their rank; and when the daughter, who was the eldest, had grown old enough to be married, he resolved to give his wife's faith another trial still. So he told her that he had grown tired of her, and wished her to return to her own house, while he would bring a new bride from a distant country.   And he bade her first prepare the palace for his wedding, and then go away forever. And Griselda said that she was ready to do his will, according to her promise.   And so he sent for his children across the sea, and Griselda, when she saw them, thought she had never seen so fair a maiden and boy, and she stood ready to serve the young bride as well as she might before she went away.   But the marquis, believing now that her heart was truly his, and that she prized his happiness more than the grand station he had given her, took her in his arms and kissed her, and told her all.   And Griselda forgot all the years of cruel suffering in the joy of her children and her husband's love, and so the story ended happily, as all stories should.

Then the Prioress, with the gentle manners and soft voice, was asked to tell a story, which she did willingly enough, using such fair speech and adorning it with such grace of delivery that all were charmed.   Her story was a sad little tale of a child who had been cruelly murdered by the Jews, because they hated to hear the songs which he sang to the Virgin as he passed to and from school. And though the deed was done in secret, and the little body had been thrown into a pit, yet his mother, led by her love, found the place out and saw the child lying there dead; and as she looked, from his lips there came forth such a beautiful song that it filled the whole place, and all the passers-by wondered. And still he sang when they bore him away to the abbey, and when the mass was said, and at last the abbot asked him to tell him the marvel, and the child said that he must sing until there was removed from his tongue a little grain which the Virgin herself had placed there, and that then she would take him to heaven. And so the abbot took away the grain and the song ceased, and all the assembled monks and nuns wept bitterly because of the death of one who was so beloved of the Virgin, and they put the child in a little marble tomb, and his story was told all over the world for a wonder and a miracle.

This story, which was thoroughly believed by all the pilgrims, was much liked by the company in spite of its sadness, for the Jews were hated all over England at that time, and the Christians liked to believe all sorts of evil about them, though why this should be so is not plain, since it was the Christians themselves who treated the Jews most cruelly, defrauding them of their money, denying them justice, and murdering them without mercy on the least occasion. Perhaps the Prioress's tale eased their consciences a little, and thus made it popular with the pilgrims.

Chaucer did not carry out his plan of having all his twenty-nine pilgrims relate one or more stories as they went and returned from Canterbury, as there are only twenty-five stories in all, and two of these are by pilgrims who joined the party after they had left the inn; but there are enough to show how rich were the imaginative powers of the poet, and as all kinds of characters were represented in the telling, the stories show exactly what each person considered necessary to the telling of a good tale. The Miller and the Cook, the Merchant and the Squire had the same chance as the Knight and the Clerk, and thus Chaucer enabled his readers to look at life from the point of view of many different characters. And it is this which gives the stories their great variety and charm, as well as makes them valuable pictures of the times which they represent.

Besides *The Canterbury Tales* Chaucer wrote several other fine poems, which are noted for their beauty. Among these are *The Flower and the Leaf, The Cuckoo and the Nightingale, The House of Fame*, and many others.

The Flower and the Leaf is an allegory representing the strength of truth and honor. A lady wanders out into a forest and seats herself in an arbor. It is a beautiful spring morning and the world is alive with fresh flowers and sweet perfumes—nightingales and goldfinches are singing all around; and while she is listening to their music she suddenly sees a band of ladies approaching. These are the servants of the Leaf. They are clothed in white, and wear garlands of laurel and woodbine, and they form a circle round one who is their queen, and sing a beautiful song, called " Under the Leaf to Me," which is interrupted by the sound of trumpets. Then appear nine knights, all armed, followed by a train of cavaliers and ladies. They joust for an hour, and then the knights lead the ladies to a large laurel-tree, to which they make obeisance. Then a third band of ladies enter, dressed in green, and led by a queen, and these do honor to a mound of flowers, and one of the ladies sings a song in praise of the daisy, which they had just made obeisance to, all the others joining in the refrain. These are the servants of the Flower. Then followed sports which were interrupted by the heat of the sun, which withered all the flowers. Then came a shower of rain, which drenched the knights and ladies of the flowers, but did not harm those who wore the leaf. Then the ladies of the Leaf pitied the ladies of the Flower, and took them by the hand and comforted them, and as the rain passed prepared a supper for them, the Queen of the Leaf entertaining the Queen of the Flowers in a friendly manner. And from the boughs above a nightingale flew down and perched on the wrist of the Lady of the Leaf, and a goldfinch came and folded his wings on the hand of the Lady of the Flower. And when supper was ended they all went away again leaving the lady in the arbor alone. The allegory shows that those who served the Flower, which typified idleness, should be overcome by the trials and storms of life, while those who served the Leaf, which signified industry and strength, should stand firm in the time of trouble.

The Cuckoo and the Nightingale is another allegory, and tells how a poet was in love with a fair lady, and how his love gave him only sorrow, for he did not know whether it was returned or not. His trouble was so great that it drove sleep from his eyes, and as he lay awake he remembered that there was an old saying that a lover who heard the nightingale's song before that of the cuckoo should be successful in his love.   The poet was charmed to think that this old proverb had come to him, for it was such an easy way to decide whether his fair lady looked upon him with favor or not; and so he rose from bed while it was yet dusk and left the house, for it was already the third of May and time for the nightingales to begin their concert of the year. He took a little brook for his guide, and it led him to a fair land where all was white and green, the grass at his feet being powdered with daisies, and the trees fresh with new leaves and the flowers gleaming white among them; and being sure that the nightingale could not help but choose such a spot to sing in, he sat down among the flowers and waited. Up among the green boughs the birds began to stir, and presently they left their pretty bowers and began singing a glad song to the day, and to the season, for birds keep Maytime as well as others. There were many beautiful voices among them, some singing cheerily, some plaintively, as if they knew the poet's woe, and others letting out their song full and rich from joy of living; and with this sweet music the voice of the little brook chimed in so melodiously that the poet was sure that there could not be heard finer music in all the world. And from very delight he fell into a gentle slumber and sweet dreaming, and in his dream he heard the song of the cuckoo right over his head. And at this he awoke full of anger and distress, for if the proverb were true the cuckoo's voice was only singing sorrow to him. And immediately afterward a nightingale's voice came out clear and beautiful from the neighboring bush, and this only increased the poet's sorrow as he had heard it too late. And while he sat there overcome with disappointment, he suddenly became conscious that he understood the voices of the birds, and could tell what they were saying to each other in their songs. And as he listened he found that the cuckoo was ridiculing love and lovers, and so the poet was glad that he had wished her to be burned with fire when her note first fell upon his ears. But the nightingale was praising love and lovers, her voice sounding so sweetly every time she answered that the poet was in greater despair than ever on account of his fair lady.

But the cuckoo could not be persuaded that love was anything but the greatest nonsense, and was so stubborn and disagreeable that at last the nightingale fell into loud weeping and cried so hard that everyone of her sweet notes sounded like a big tear falling on the ground, and at this the poet became so enraged with the cuckoo that he caught up a big stone and threw it at her, and drove her away, and told the nightingale not to mind, for he had heard it all and was quite of her opinion that love was the chief thing in the world; and then he sighed so dismally that the nightingale was touched with pity, and in her gratitude promised to be his singer all through the month of May, and said that she knew of a charm that would undo the cuckoo's note, and that if he used it well he might win his fair lady after all. The charm was that he was to go and look every day upon the daisy that held a magic power, provided those who looked upon it were good and true, and would bring all their wishes to them if they were faithful. And with this comfort the night-ingale left the poet, and flew up and down the green dale, and called all the birds together, and told them how she had been treated by the cuckoo. And all the birds agreed that it was a matter that needed serious attention, and they decided to call a parliament of birds, choose the eagle for judge, and summon the cuckoo to appear and answer the nightingale's charge. And they furthermore agreed that the parliament should be held the day after St. Valentine's day, and that the place of meeting should be in a fair green maple-tree. And then the nightingale thanked them and flew back to her hawthorn bush, and began singing again of love, in a voice so clear and loud that the poet awoke.

The House of Fame is a poem in the form of a dream, in which Chaucer sees all the heroes and heroines of the world who had been in any way famous. Chaucer dreams that he is standing in a temple of glass, on the walls of which were golden images and portraits of all those lovers whose histories were written by the old poets, for this was the temple of Venus. And

being bewildered with the vision he went outside to find someone who would tell him where
he was; and as he looked upward he saw a
great eagle, whose plumage shone like gold in
the sun, coming toward him, and it caught him
up and bore him far away from the glass temple
and the shifting sands on which it stood, carrying him high in the air, where he passed
through clouds, and mists, and snow, and hail,
and rain, and heard the voices of the winds and
tempests, and saw the stars in their near glory,
and other mysteries of the heavens, coming at
last to the House of Fame, where the eagle left
him.   The House of Fame stood on rocks of
ice, on which were written the names of all who
had wished for fame; and some names were
fast melting away, but others remained as fresh
as when first graven.   The castle itself was
of beryl, full of shining windows, and crowned
with turrets, in which stood Orpheus, and Arion,
and all the great musicians who once charmed
the earth with their sweet music, and with these
great harpers stood crowds of other musicians,
who made constant music on horns, flutes,

and reeds, so that the air was sweet with melody.

And as he entered the temple, which was covered with plates of gold, he saw a beautiful queen sitting on a throne made of one great carbuncle, and so great was the majesty of her person that her form seemed to reach up to heaven, and her winged feet rested on a foot-stool of gold embossed with gems, and her eyes were like stars for brilliancy and seemed to see even men's thoughts. And by her stood a great crowd of heralds, whose cloaks were embroidered with the names of the most famous knights in history, and the temple was full of the music relating the great deeds they had done. And upon metal pillars stood the statues of all the great poets and historians. Josephus, the historian of the Jews, upon a pillar of lead; Statius, the historian, upon a pillar of iron stained with tigers' blood; Ovid, the Roman, on a pillar of copper, and higher than the rest, on a pillar of iron, stood the great Homer. And then there was Virgil, and Livy, and Geoffrey of Monmouth, and hosts of others, who all stood there for sake of fame in song and story. And there came before the queen, who was the Goddess of Fame, many different persons, who knelt and asked boons of her, and some she granted and others she refused. Some who asked for fame were denied; some who had done noble deeds asked to be forgotten, as they had worked for Truth's sake alone, and this she granted to some, and to others she refused, and had their deeds trumpeted aloud through a golden clarion; and so on, for the queen was continually hearing requests and granting or refusing them. And then the dreamer was taken by the eagle to the House of Rumor, near by, where every tale told of loss or gain, or sorrow or joy, in all the world, was reported by messengers as soon as they heard it, so that there was nothing that happened on the earth that was not immediately reported here. And the noise of all this woke the poet up, and he saw that it had all been a dream.

Chaucer wrote so many poems that it would take a whole book to tell about them all; and although many of his stories were simply tales from other writers retold in English, yet he put them to such beautiful music and clothed them in such rich dress that they seem his very own. *The Canterbury Tales* are considered his finest work, and show best his great power as a poet. His poems were written in the English which was spoken by the nobility and upper classes, and thus differs from that of Langlande who wrote the English of the peasants, which was almost untouched by French influence. Yet because Chaucer thus put his great poems into the language of the day, and gave it a fixed form, he is often called the father of English poetry, though at the time he wrote, the language he used was that of the court and city, rather than of the nation at large. He died in 1400 and was buried in Westminster Abbey.

CHAPTER XI.

The third great name in English literature during the fourteenth century, that of John Wickliffe, belongs to the priesthood, and makes the representation of each great class of life by some great writer complete—Chaucer standing for the higher classes, Langlande for the people, and Wickliffe for the Church.

The Vision of Piers Plowman, which showed in the form of a dream all the evils that England was suffering, bitterly accused the Church for the part it had in the troubles. And this was one reason of its great popularity among the common people. The great nobles, and the wealthy abbots who were supported by the toil of the poor, had to bear in return the ill-will of those whom they oppressed, though as a rule this dislike was often hidden through fear. It was only when some song or word against the clergy became instantly popular and spread all over the country like wildfire that this hatred and the great power of it were perceived.

Thus in the ballades of Robin Hood, the people were always delighted when some monk or friar was the object of ridicule, and nothing did so much to make Robin himself a hero among the yeomanry and peasants as his hatred of priests. This was because the Church, instead of following the principles and practice of its Founder, was busy about getting great grants of land, and building huge monasteries, and fine churches, and cathedrals; and the priesthood, which had first won England from barbarism by preaching love and kindness, and by lives of self-denial and hardship, was now represented by men who thought only of being well fed and well clothed, and whose sermons were often only a means of getting money from the poor.

Langlande saw this, and his poem had its greatest power because it seemed to speak right from the hearts of the suffering people, thus showing him to be a true poet, for it is only such that can translate a thought into words, and make just such a poem as the people themselves would have made if they had had the gift of song. And Chaucer saw it too, and while he wrote pretty allegories of birds and flowers, and painted English life in *The Canterbury Tales* in colors that can never fade, he did not fail to show the selfishness of the priests, and their love of ease and riches. But although things were in this state they were not utterly hopeless, for there were yet many men among the priests who loved truth and justice and lived noble lives. Langlande himself was one of these, and there was another who was equally famous both as a reformer and writer. This was John Wickliffe, who was born in 1324, in the village of Wickliffe in Yorkshire, and who died after a well-spent life sixty years after.

Among his other descriptions in *The Canterbury Tales* Chaucer has given one of a good priest, who was poor in worldly goods but rich in "holy thought and work," and who, though learned and wise, devoted his great knowledge

to the winning of men from evil, who gave of
the little money he had to those who were
poorer still, and who rode not on a richly capa-
risoned horse, but, staff in hand, walked from
house to house of his widely scattered parish,
bringing comfort to the sick, brotherly kindness
to the well, and good to all. And it has been
supposed that this picture of a noble priest was
drawn from the character of John Wickliffe.
Whether this be true or not matters little, the
real interest in the description lying in the fact
that such priests were possible even in those
times, and that it was by their efforts the nation
was saved from losing all faith in religion.

Nothing is known of Wickliffe's childhood,
but if he belonged to the family of Wickliffe who
were lords of the manor from the time of the
Conquest, he must have had the careful nurture
and training which was usual in wealthy families.
When he was about sixteen he entered Oxford
College, which had been founded by Queen
Philippa a short time before, and from this time
his life was that of a student of books. And
while Chaucer was fighting in the army of Ed-

ward III., and practising a courtier's arts at the court, and while Langlande was living in poverty in London, and learning, by the experience of the poor, the wants of the poor, Wickliffe was studying only books—books that had been written a thousand and more years before by Greeks and Romans, books that had been written hundreds of years before by Italians, French, Germans, and Englishmen, and books that were then being written by living men who were renowned for their learning. But as the time came for Langlande to write the sad song which the people were singing in their hearts, and for Chaucer to paint English society in words which formed the English language, so it came for Wickliffe to leave off his study of books and speak to the nation such words as they were not used to hearing from the lips of a priest; and the time found him ready. And though it is good to know that Langlande spoke truth because he was a peasant and knew the peasant's life, and that Chaucer spoke truth because he was a courtier as well as a poet and knew that life, it is still better to know that Wickliffe spoke truth because he was a priest, for it shows that even then, in those dark days, the Church had not lost sight of the divine light which it had first followed when it first preached the doctrine of the equality of man.

Wickliffe's first important work as a reformer was his public protest against the begging friars who were then overrunning England. These begging friars, or, as they are generally called, mendicant brotherhoods, came into existence about a hundred years before the birth of Wickliffe, and at first did noble work for the cause of religion. The Church at that time was very rich and powerful, and many people had lost faith in religion because the priests led lives of indolence and selfishness. It was then that a few noble souls saw that Christianity would soon become a thing of ridicule to the whole world unless some change took place in the priesthood. And so, as this thought came to one and another, religious orders were formed which consisted only of men who took vows of poverty and self-denial, and as these orders thus practised what the first Christians had taught and practised, they speedily became famous, and their numbers increased rapidly. There is no doubt that the mendicant orders, when first established, did a great service for the Church, for the brothers led pure lives, kept strictly to their vow of poverty, and in all ways showed themselves sincere followers of their Master.

But in the course of a hundred years the begging friars had become so numerous and powerful, that they, in turn, almost forgot the old precepts of their order, and many of them became as greedy of wealth and as selfish in their lives as the priests they had first waged war against. They had immense revenues, owned vast estates, and exercised great influence in the affairs of state and of private life. They robbed the poor by threats of future punishment, unless they gave them their little earnings, and they promised forgiveness to the rich if they would only give large sums of money to their order. Even the Church itself at last grew afraid of the begging friars, and of their bad effect upon religion, and took measures to lessen their power long before the time of Wickliffe. During the

time of Edward III. the friars were exceedingly
unpopular, and were doubly hated when it was
found that they had succeeded in persuading
the students of the universities to join their
order in great numbers, as a result of which
Oxford alone had lost four-fifths of its students,
who were taken away by their guardians from
an influence so undesirable.

Owing to this a law was passed that no youth
under eighteen should be permitted to join the
mendicants, and this blow to their power was
followed by a crusade against them, which was
led by the most important and thoughtful men
of the age. Wickliffe could not fail to be among
those who entered heart and soul into this
great reform, and his tracts against the mendicant orders soon made his name famous
throughout Christendom. His influence was
most powerful because of his great eloquence
and masterly arguments, and because he was
known to be absolutely fearless in the cause of
the right, and incapable of being influenced by
offers of wealth or power to abandon that cause.
This course had two very opposite results for

14

Wickliffe.   In the first place, it gave him the position of the first reformer of the age, and finally led to his appointment as Professor of Divinity at Oxford; and in the second place, because he kept up his character of reformer, and constantly raised his voice against all abuses, it led to his banishment from Oxford when it was found that he not only attacked the begging friars, but was equally ready to point out the wrongs which existed in the Church itself.

But his banishment, which his enemies regarded as well-deserved defeat, was really the means of enabling him to perform the great work of his life.   For although Wickliffe's writings against the corruptions of the Church were of great value, and placed him among the world's great reformers, it was work of another kind which has given him his place in English literature, and a fame that grows brighter with every age.   This was the translation of the Bible into the English tongue, a work which was a glorious crowning to the literature of the fourteenth century.   From Oxford Wickliffe went to the parish of Lutterworth, and it was while in this obscure place, and while performing the duties of a parish priest, that he began the great work which has been full of such mighty results to the English race.

One of the chief causes of the great success of the mendicants lay in the fact that they preached to the people in English, unlike the regular clergy, who still kept up the old traditions of the Church by delivering sermons in the Latin tongue. Wickliffe, while despising the begging friars, still saw that they had taken the true way to reach the hearts of the people, and followed their example in using English in the services of the Church. And it was perhaps this which first suggested to him the great gain that would follow to the cause of religion if it were possible for the people to read the Bible in English; for it seemed to him that the book which was considered to teach the articles of the Christian faith should be open to all who cared to read its pages. Up to this time but a small portion of the Bible had ever been translated into the common tongue, though at different times some portions had been made familiar to the people by the *paraphrases*, or poetic renderings, and others by literal translation.

Cædmon's paraphrase was the earliest attempt to put the Bible story into English, and this was not a translation, but a religious poem in which the events described were taken from the Bible. Bede and King Alfred translated some parts of the Bible, and other writers after them put various portions into the language of the people—Saxon, Anglo-Norman, or English being used, according to the time in which the author lived. These translations, or paraphrases, were often written on finest vellum and beautifully illustrated, or illuminated, with the gorgeous colored letters and pictures that the old monks loved to execute, and they were regarded as great treasures by the churches or monasteries which possessed them. But they still seemed only meant to enrich the libraries of the monks, and were almost unknown to the nation at large, which learned nearly all that it knew of the Bible from the pictures in the churches and the stories of the Gospels as re-peated by some one familiar with Latin.

And thus the work of giving the whole Bible to the English people, in such a way that it could serve for their guide in religion, was yet undone, and this work Wickliffe determined should be his. And so he found time, in the midst of many other duties, to retire every day to his little study at Lutterworth, and give a portion of his time to the translation of the Bible into English, finding more pleasure in the thought that by so doing he might be the means of leading the poor peasants to a higher life, than in the knowledge that the same pen which put the simple Gospel stories into the common tongue, was feared alike by Pope and clergy as the most powerful weapon that they were called upon to resist.

This great work could hardly have been undertaken by Wickliffe alone, for he was then sixty years of age, and his health was far from good. It is probable, therefore, that he was assisted in his task by some of the younger priests and laymen who were constantly around him, attracted by the sincerity of his life and doctrines. The little vicarage of Lutterworth, in-

deed, must have somewhat resembled the scrip-
toriums of the old monasteries, where monk and
novice wrought their silent task, and Wickliffe,
like Bede, must have sat surrounded by his faithful pupils, who followed his instructions with
loving care and treasured his words beyond all
the jewels that blazed on the costly covers of
the volumes that were valueless to the people
because written in the Latin tongue.

One would think that a translation of the book
which the Church professed to follow for her
guide would have been eagerly welcomed by all
true Christians, but this was far from the case,
and Wickliffe had to endure greater persecution
than ever, while the new English Bible was de-
nounced by the Church as an enemy to religion
and all who read it were looked upon with dis-
approval, because the Church claimed the exclusive right of interpreting Scripture and therefore
opposed people's doing this for themselves. But
Wickliffe only persevered in his course, and sent
as many Bibles abroad as his means would allow.
One copy after another was made, and his followers eagerly studied the new message which

it brought, and read it aloud to the people in the little chapels where the disciples of Wickliffe gathered. And the seed thus scattered bore such rich harvests that in ten years' time the Church found it necessary to induce Parliament to pass a law forbidding the reading of Wickliffe's Bible. But hundreds of persons suffered imprisonment and death rather than obey this law, and from the time of the first appearance of the English Bible its influence remained unbounded, in spite of the powerful opposition of the Church and the hatred of Wickliffe's enemies.

Wickliffe was greatly assisted, both in proclaiming his views of reform and in spreading the Bible, by a class of men whom he called his "poor priests." These were not always regular priests, but were generally sincere and earnest men who wished to spread the truth abroad and who took every opportunity to preach the doctrines of Wickliffe. Their numbers increased rapidly, and, like the begging friars, they wandered over England from place to place for the good of their cause. Only, unlike the friars then, though like them as they were at first, they really gave up their lives to poverty and hardship, having no rich monasteries to retreat to when their working-days were over, and scorning to take from the poor that which they needed for their own support.   These men wore coarse clothing, and lived on the poorest fare, were always ready to deny themselves of even the necessaries of life if they found another's need greater than their own, and looking upon churches and temples as of little account if they were not the refuge of the poor, they preached their faith in the halls of private houses, in barns, or on the highway, at fairs and market-places, and wherever they could find men and women to listen to them.

It was a new thing to England at that time to have religion offered free, and the " poor priests " became instantly popular among the people, winning both their respect and love by their brave and self-denying labors.   And among the many pictures which England showed in the fourteenth century there was none more interesting and full of vital meaning than that of the great fair or market-day, where, amid buying and selling, bargaining, horse-trading, singing, shouting, and the exhibitions of jugglers and showmen of every kind, there could be seen the figure of one of Wickliffe's "poor priests," his coarse robe in strange contrast to the holiday garments of the others, and his face lighted up with holy enthusiasm, as he spoke to a little circle of curious listeners, and told them of the new doctrine of a free religion, of the gift of Wickliffe's Bible, and above all of the equality of rich and poor in the true brotherhood which was preached by the new faith.

As might have been expected, the "poor priests" met with much opposition and persecution on account of the doctrines they taught. The church tried in every way to suppress them, and even the people themselves were not always willing to listen to their preaching, and believed that anything that the church proscribed must be wrong, no matter how reasonable or just it might seem. But in spite of threats, and cursing, and stoning, they kept on with their work, and by their unremitting toil Wickliffe's doctrines and the English Bible became familiar throughout all England, while their numbers increased so rapidly that it became a common saying that a man could not meet two people on the road without knowing that one of them was a " poor priest."

Besides the effect which the English Bible had upon the character of the English nation at one of its most important periods, its influence upon the language is inestimable, as it helped fix it in the highest form it had reached, and if no other book had been written in English during the fourteenth century, it alone would have been sufficient to give permanence to the mother tongue, and raise it from a dialect to the place that it thereafter held.

And if to Chaucer belongs the honor of having given to the English language a strong, beautiful, and living body, to Wickliffe belongs the equal glory of endowing that body with a soul whose divine presence has never ceased to turn the hearts of men to pure ideals and high purposes.　The Bible is the one book to which, through all succeeding centuries and in the midst of powerful rivals, the English race has turned as its hope and inspiration, and which has moulded the thought of one of the greatest nations of all time. And that this is so is due largely to the efforts of Wickliffe, who, in his study at Lutterworth, thought only of giving to the English peasants the Bible in their native tongue, little dreaming that the seed he was sowing should yield such rich harvests. In the sixteenth century, Wickliffe's Bible was made the basis of two versions by the reformers Tyndale and Coverdale, and these, in turn, were the foundation of the version authorized by King James in 1611, and which is still in use.

CHAPTER XII.

CAXTON.

During the century that followed the death of Chaucer no writer appeared who could worthily be called his successor, and it seemed that English literature, which had risen to such a height in the fourteenth century, was destined in the fifteenth to remain almost stationary, as far as the writing of any great book or poem was concerned, although men knew that the music which Chaucer had sung must in time be carried on by other voices, perhaps as melodious as his.

For nearly a hundred years the cloud of civil war hung over the land, and the best blood of England was poured in lavish measure on the battlefields which marked the progress of the Wars of the Roses. The splendid pageants, courts of love, tournaments, and chivalric amusements which distinguished the Court of Edward III. gave place to the confusion and strife of contending aspirants to the throne, the noise of fateful battles, and that unrest, discomfort and misery which abound even in palaces when a nation is divided against itself; for not only did the people suffer as greatly as when their woes were sung by Langlande, but the nobility now felt the touch of a cruel fate, and the whole of England was overborne by the weight of a trouble unrelieved even by such a show of gorgeous colors as had tinged the courtly side of society when Wickliffe and Langlande undertook to lift the lower classes into fairer ways of life. But yet, strange as it may seem, although the men who in time of peace might have been holding the pen were wielding sword and battle-ax, and English literature, like an unfinished song, was awaiting some one to take up the interrupted melody, it was at this very period that an event occurred which gave to books and education an impetus that carried them into wider ways than any they had yet found and by which book-making progressed at a rate unparalleled in the history of any other art. This was the introduction of printing, which brought about a revolution whose effects it is impossible to overestimate, and conferred upon the common people a more priceless gift than any ever bestowed by king or conqueror.

The oldest nations of which we have any record used some means of preserving their histories long before written volumes existed, and at a time when man had not yet thought of expressing his ideas in written words. During these periods the methods used differed very much, according to the nature and condition of the people, and if these historical records could be all gathered together in one place they would show so much individuality that it would be easy to distinguish the work of different nations, and read their several histories, even at this distance of time. But long before even the rudest attempts to record history, each tribe or nation preserved its traditions by transmitting them orally from one generation to another. This method, of course, was very imperfect, as it was so liable to allow errors to creep in. And so, almost from necessity, it became the custom, when any event of great importance happened, to endeavor to record it in some way less subject to change than oral tradition.

This would be done by those of the tribe who possessed the gift of representing any natural object by drawing or carving, and as this method became more and more popular there came to be a recognized class of men whose chief business was to preserve the history of the people by making pictures or rude sculptures of their battles, victories, defeats, and other eventful episodes. This method was kept up often long after the people possessed a language rich enough to express every thought in a poetical way, for there was a great difference between picture-making, which stood for some person or event, and writing, which stood for spoken speech.

Thus the North American Indians, whose language was so rich that its beautiful imagery charmed their European listeners, were content always to write their histories in pictures, graven sometimes on rocks, sometimes portrayed on tanned skins, but always limited to the simplest representation which could be devised. Thus a great war, which had resulted perhaps in the total extinction of a powerful tribe, and which may have changed the history of these savage people, would be represented perhaps simply by a picture of the conquering chief holding in his hand the scalp of a warrior of the defeated tribe, accompanied by some hieroglyphic signs to show in what year it occurred, and giving no account of the meetings, war-councils, and preparations which preceded the strife, though those very council meetings gave rise to some of the finest of that oratory for which the Indians were so celebrated.

The old nations had at first only this kind of picture-writing; but from picture-making to word-making, though a very long process in point of time, was but a simple one really. The first written words stood only for the pictures that had formerly been used, and written language at first was as unadorned and primitive as the picture language, a whole word being expressed by a single letter, which had been modified from the picture itself. These characters were imprinted on implements, arms, coins, gems, public buildings, tombs, and pillars, and, together with a rude painting or sculpture of some important event, made up the recorded history of the early ages of civilization. Gradually, however, a written language, corresponding to speech itself, came into being, and then the making of books properly began.

The first books were written upon many different kinds of material, according to the time or country in which they were made. In some places the leaves of the trees were used for writing upon, those of the mallow and palm particularly, and these were sometimes pasted together at the edges to form a larger surface. It is probable, however, that leaves were not used for making historical records, or for any writing that was meant to endure, as they were too fragile to admit of such use ; and these leaf-books were in all likelihood used only for teaching, or for business purposes and the sending of official messages. The bark of trees was also used for these first books, the inner bark of the linden coming into such general favor that its name, *liber* in Latin and *biblos* in Greek, came to stand for the word book in both languages.   But this was also, like the leaves, subject to injury and decay, and the most important documents were written on some other substance.   Sometimes they were graven on pillars in palaces and public halls, and sometimes on tables of solid wood.   These wooden tables, called *codices*, were used chiefly for legal documents, and, as in the case of the bark, a set of laws came in time to be called a code, from the *codex*, or table of wood on which it was written.

Among the Greeks and Romans leaves and tablets of lead and ivory, covered with wax, were also used for writing; the pen, which was called a stylus, being made of iron, brass, ivory, bone, or wood, and having the upper end flat for the purpose of scratching off the wax when it was necessary.   These tablets were always carried around everywhere, and there is a statute of one of the Roman emperors which forbids the use of the iron stylus, as it was sometimes used as a weapon of defence or attack by its owner.

But the material which was, after a time, used almost universally by the old writers was parchment, or prepared skin, called also *pergamena*, from Pergamos, in Asia Minor, where it was largely prepared. This was a costly material because of the expense and time it took to prepare it. Pens made of reeds were used in writing upon it, and it was possible, from the nature of both the material and the ink employed, to erase the writing and use it for a new book.

These parchments were sometimes dyed red or yellow, and one of the most ancient manuscripts of the Bible is upon crimson leather. The skins thus used were cut into strips of the required length, sometimes of one hundred feet, and these were connected together so as to contain an entire work; they were rolled up and tied when not in use, and our word volume comes from the Latin *volumen*, meaning a roll. But during many ages the material most in use for making books was papyrus, which formed the substance of nearly all books until paper came in use, though parchment never went out of use; and, indeed, when in time the supply of

papyrus became exhausted, was still the re-
source of the book-maker.

The papyrus was a plant which grew in immense quantities in the stagnant pools that
were formed by the overflowing of the Nile,
and as the Egyptians worshipped this river as
a god, because its inundations moistened the
soil and brought their grain to perfection, thus
supplying them with the means of life, so they
also regarded with grateful veneration the gift
which enabled them to preserve their history;
for of all the ancient nations they were the most
given to preserving the memory of their deeds
and achievements. Their kings built great
tombs, sculptured sphinxes, and raised pyramids
which have been the wonder of all succeeding
ages, to commemorate their glory ; and next to
the wheat which ripened on the muddy bottoms
left by the subsiding Nile, they prized the plant
which their priests and scholars used for making
books. For though every part of the papyrus
was used for something, the lower part being
formed into cups and other household utensils,
the pith used as food, and the fibrous parts

formed into cloth, shoes, baskets, lamp-wicks, sails for ships, and other articles, it was the paper produced from it that gave it its chief value.

The process of preparation consisted in peeling off the coat its entire length, moistening it with the juice which was expressed, and, after laying it across a block of wood, placing another layer upon it. The two layers, thus cemented by the juice, were pressed, dried in the sun, beaten smooth with a broad mallet, and then, last of all, polished carefully with a shell. It was then considered ready for use. Papyrus was a source of great wealth to the Egyptians for centuries, immense quantities being sent annually to Greece, Rome, and other countries, and it is no wonder that the natives prized so highly a plant which combined so many virtues, and which could be used either as an article of food, made into a bed to sleep upon, or converted into sails to bear the paper across the Mediterranean; while the leaves from the same plant were woven into garlands and placed on the shrines of the gods, with the prayers that the voyagers might come safely home again.

The art of paper-making from papyrus was brought to the greatest perfection by the Romans after the subjugation of Egypt by that power, and they developed a paper of exquisite whiteness and smoothness. But the greatest care could not discover a way of making this paper as strong as parchment, and it became the custom to insert leaves of parchment here and there between the brittle leaves of papyrus, the most ancient books thus often being made of the two materials. The ink used in writing these old books is supposed to have been made of soot, powdered coals of ivory, and fine woods, mixed with gums. There were also gold, silver, red, and blue inks, and a purple dye used for the royal decrees, and called the sacred encaustic. Sometimes the titles of the chapters were written in alternate red and blue, the marginal notes in another color, and whole pages in gold and silver, thus making the book look like a beautiful picture. The gold and silver inks were chiefly used for religious books, and among the oldest books is a copy of the Gospels written on purple parchment, with letters of gold throughout, thus expressing the idea of the old scribes that no medium could be too costly to convey the precious gift of thought.

The pens used in writing with ink were made of reeds and rushes chiefly, though the quill was sometimes preferred. A pen of this kind was called a *calamus*, from the Latin name of the reed used. These instruments of writing often served as a sign of the profession of the scribe; and the scalpel for trimming the pen, the compass for measuring the lines, and the scissors for cutting the paper, were always on the desks of ancient writers, and figure in all the pictures relating to early book-making. After a time papyrus became very scarce, and book-making, which was then a recognized art among all civilized nations, was in danger of declining, owing to the lack of paper. Parchment, which had always been a very expensive material, increased greatly in value, and it became a serious matter to undertake to write an entirely new book.

And besides this, another reason caused the making of books almost to cease, and this was the political condition of Europe; for it was during the period when ignorance abounded everywhere, owing to the feudal system, which divided every country of Europe up into so many military states, and left all arts, except that of fighting, to fall into disuse and disfavor. During this time—between the ninth and fourteenth centuries—a very curious custom came into use in regard to book-making. Learning was almost entirely in the hands of the priests, and books were the almost exclusive property of the monasteries, and the scarcity of paper from papyrus, and the great expense of parchment, led the monks to take advantage of the fact that writing on parchment could be erased, and to put the old manuscripts to new uses. Thus many valuable works were entirely lost when it was possible to erase completely the original writing.

But, in spite of chemicals and scrubbing, the parchment often retained the imprint of the earlier book, and a volume which had had the curious experience of bearing first the imprint of some Greek or Latin classic, and secondly the life of the favorite saint of some mediæval scribe, was often deciphered long afterward by some earnest student, and its first imprint brought to light.

Still, although books suffered in this way at the hands of the old monks, it is to them alone that we owe the preservation of the libraries during this time. And when learning had almost entirely disappeared, the monasteries and religious houses still kept their treasured manuscripts, and abbot and novice guarded alike, as their most precious possession, the costly gifts of thought whose price could not be valued in gold or silver. And it was fortunate that this was the case, for in those times of disorder and change the monasteries alone were secure from disturbance, and books were safer there than they would have been in kings' palaces, from conquest and revolution. And while one form of power succeeded to another, and different dynasties passed away, the property of the monasteries still remained in possession of the religious orders, and was passed down from age to age undisputed, and guarded with loyal devotion.

And so the work of book-making went on in the midst of the tumult of war and the darkness of superstition, and the old scribes copied patiently and faithfully their appointed stint, and did it right honestly, as may be proven by the fact that after a thousand and more years the various copies, made at different times and places, show only those slight variations which would be due to the mechanical part of the work, and that the text remains, word for word, almost identical, only the date at the end, and the name of the copyist and king, giving distinction to the work. These monasteries were scattered all over Christendom, and some of them became specially noted for their work of transcription. Among the most famous places for making books in those old times was Mount Athos, the whole sides of the mountain being covered with religious houses; and when it came time to trace out the history of the old manuscripts, and learn their date of transcription, this place speedily became renowned for its valuable literary treasures, a renown which it enjoys to this day.

In determining the age of these old manuscripts many different things are taken into account—such as whether they were written on paper, papyrus, or parchment; what kind of ink was used, and the character of the illuminations; and so expert have students become in this branch of research that it is almost as easy to determine the age of a manuscript, buried perhaps for centuries beneath some ruined monastery, as to reckon the relative ages of rocks by the fossils they contain. And the antiquity of some of these books is indeed remarkable, considering their fragile nature and the continual risks to which they were subject, and much of the ancient learning must have been lost to the world but for its preservation in this very way. For when the famous libraries of Alexandria, Constantinople, Rome, Athens, and other places were destroyed, the classic writers were so diffused that they were known in all parts of Western Europe and Asia, and the religious orders, holding this knowledge as their chief treasure, transmitted it by copy to future generations, and kept alive the lamp of learning which was so perilously near extinction during the Dark Ages. Thus we owe a precious debt to these old monks, who, working so patiently for the cause of knowledge and the glory of their order, perhaps may have had a vision of the time to come when the walls of their monasteries would lie in ruins, and they themselves be only remembered by the volumes whose gold and jewelled covers still glittered brightly, though the dust of centuries had hidden them from view.

Just as the scarcity of papyrus and the costliness of parchment began to be seriously felt in the art of book-making, an event occurred which marked a new era in the manufacture of books, and made it possible for every library to possess as many as the number and skill of their scribes or copyists would permit. This was the introduction of paper made from cotton, which had been used for some time in the East, and which made its appearance in Europe at a most opportune time, becoming comparatively cheap and within the reach of all when it was discovered that it could be manufactured from old rags.

From the time that paper was introduced the number of manuscripts increased at a more rapid rate than ever before, as one great cause of their scarcity—the cost of material—was removed. But as learning was still almost entirely confined to the monastic orders, the manuscripts for the most part still remained the property of the monasteries. Books were loaned from one college to another, and from one monastery to another, only on condition that a duplicate of the work remained at home ; and if any great scholar bequeathed a few books at his death to a favorite college, they were carefully deposited in chests and jealously guarded by students set apart for that purpose.

The books in use were generally chained to the desks, and a curious old college law of this time proclaims that no scholar shall have the use of a book for more than an hour at a time, or two hours on a special occasion. Even at this period of comparative cheapness, books were so scarce that kings were glad to borrow them from the churches and universities, and, if we are to believe the old records, they were sometimes not returned; while an illuminated manuscript, decorated with gold and silver pictures and initials, and bound in velvet or silk, and adorned with lace, tassels, and jewels, was thought to be the price of a prince's ransom, and to stand for the most valuable booty taken in battle. Still, books were sometimes bought and sold, and after a time there even grew up a custom among the booksellers of having books to hire, though the reading class still consisted almost entirely of priests and lawyers, and the people at large regarded books as things entirely out of their line, and the possession of learning almost of the same nature as the possession of the black art.

But all this time the day was coming nearer when, in place of the few books which were sent out at long intervals by the monasteries and universities, there would be thousands of printing-presses all over the world, sending out books in almost countless numbers, so that whoever would might read, and the wisdom of the greatest scholars become the property of the poorest peasant.   There have been many disputes as to what nation may claim the honor of the invention of printing, and learned men have written books and treatises to show that the glory belongs to this or that country.   But it will probably never be known who first conceived the idea of making a carved block do the work of the hand, and imprinting from it words and sentences.   And as written language is the heritage of all civilized nations, and arose probably among each one independently, so it is very likely that the idea of a printed language may have occurred to more than one mind at the same time, a thing which would be quite in keeping with the histories of many other discoveries and inventions.

We know that the art of printing from blocks was practised in the early part of the Christian era by the people of the East, for in the year 175 A.D. the text of some of the Chinese classics was cut in tablets erected outside the royal university, and that impressions were taken from them.   It is also known that in the year 675 A.D. a Japanese emperor had a million toy pagodas made for the temples, each of which contained quotations from the holy books, printed on paper ; and that in the eleventh century the Chinese knew the art of printing with movable clay types.

It is maintained by some that the art of printing was brought to Europe from the East by sailors, and that the West owes this, together with the cultivation of the silkworm and many other gifts, to the old Asiatic nations ; but, however this may be, it is only idle to discuss it, as the time is too remote and the proofs are too meagre to make such discussion profitable.   It is sufficient for us to believe that printing, as a modern art, first appeared in Germany in the fifteenth century, being invented by John Gutenberg, a citizen of Mainz, assisted by John Faust, a fellow-citizen, and perfected by Peter Schoeffer, son-in-law to Faust, though opinions vary greatly as to who should have the greatest honor in bringing the new invention to light, and each of the three has been at various times honored with the title of inventor of printing.

Gutenberg had to build upon the printing of legends, texts, and religious pictures from carved blocks, the stencilling of playing-cards, and the making of *block-books*, so called because they were little books of forty or fifty leaves, each leaf containing a wood-cut or some extract from the Scriptures, the whole page being imprinted from an engraved block of the same size. Each block contained one page; thick ink was used, which did not spread, and the two pages were often pasted together. These wooden pages took up great space, and could be used for nothing else.

These processes were already in use and here was the germ of modern printing, and Gutenberg had but to work from this to something larger. The next step from an engraved or carved block, containing a legend, would be the idea that, instead of a block with a whole word carved upon it, there might be a block which had but one letter, and that this letter could be used, with other single letters, to form, first, a Scripture text; next, a line from the classic poets, and so on indefinitely; and this process of having separate letters or movable types contains the whole of printing.

It seems a very easy transition to look upon now; but it stands for many years of toil and discouragement by the old wood-carvers who worked at it so patiently. Gutenberg spent the best years of his life and all his property in developing the idea, and but for the help of Faust would have abandoned it altogether for lack of means; for all the different experiments with wood, copper, and tin blocks and types, cost much money, and in those days money was a rare possession for a man in Gutenberg's class in life. It is said that the invention of cutting the forms of all the letters of the alphabet, so that each letter might be singly cast in copper or tin, belongs to Schoeffer, who first cut the letters in wooden matrixes, and then had the whole alphabet cast, keeping it a secret until the work was complete. At first these metal letters were hardly as successful as the carved wooden ones; but as at last a means was discovered of mixing the metal with some substance which made it hard enough to stand the necessary pressure, they came into general use, and the art of printing from movable types was an accomplished fact.

The invention was kept a secret for a long time, every workman taking an oath of secrecy; but after the sacking of Mainz, in the war that soon followed, many of the inhabitants fled to different countries, and among them were some of the printers, who continued to practise the art in their new homes, and thus made printing universally known. Printers' guilds soon sprang up in Rome, Paris, Lyons, Venice, and other great cities, each city vying with the rest in the number and beauty of its books, and everywhere the printer was received with honor as the possessor of a marvellous gift.

These first printed books were sometimes very curious, and as far as beauty was concerned were much inferior to the beautiful illuminated manuscripts familiar to scholars. The pages were without title, number, or paragraph, and the words were so close together that it was difficult to read them. The letters were all of the same size. No capitals were used for the beginning of sentences or proper names, and blanks were left for the titles, initial letters, and other ornaments to be supplied by the illuminator. These adornments consisted of gold and silver letters, and figures of saints, birds, flowers, and other designs in the margins, as in the old manuscripts. When it was necessary to quote Greek, a space was left for the scribe to perform this work, as there was no type to correspond. There were no tables of contents, and when the printer's name was used it was put at the end of the book, with a text from Scripture accompanying it. The spelling in these old books varied with almost every printer, and so many abbreviations were used that at length there had to be a whole book written to explain them.

The art of printing was for a long time considered almost as magic art, so deep a reverence did the people have for the new process of multiplying books at such a rapid rate. There is a story told that Faust, before the secret was divulged, printed a number of Bibles in which the letters were so like hand-work,

and the titles and capitals so beautifully illuminated that they sold for an immense sum; but
that the honest burghers, finding a greater number of copies in his possession than it would
have been possible for many men to transcribe
in a lifetime, and the pages of each copy so exactly alike, arrested him for sorcery, and it was
only by disclosing the secret that he was allowed to go. Whether this story be true or not,
it might easily have been the experience of
one of the first printers, and well illustrates the
character of the times in which they lived,
when a few manuscripts were considered a worthy dower for a nobleman's daughter, and the
possession of ever so small a library implied a
royal revenue.

This wonderful new art was brought into
England by William Caxton, a merchant, who
was living abroad, and who, it is supposed,
learned printing from some workman of Faust
or Gutenberg, who left Mainz after its down-
fall. Caxton was born in the year 1410, in
Kent, England, and was the son of a yeoman.
Although born after the death of Chaucer, and

therefore heir to the new-formed language which he did so much to fix, Caxton's home was so far from London, and the great centres of commerce and learning, that it is doubtful whether the English of Chaucer was at all familiar to him in his youth ; for the places remote from London, and having but little communication with it, would be the last to feel the influence of any new thought, and would keep to the old ways long after they had fallen into disuse in the large cities.

Caxton himself said that the English which was spoken in Kent when he was a boy differed very much from that used at the court; and when, in after years, he found it necessary to put his thoughts and experience into written language, or was engaged about translating the works of others into his own tongue, he made continual allusions to his early education, praying that all defects might be excused because of the disadvantages which he suffered in childhood, when the Kentish country people still used the old words and pronounced English so differently from the people of the cities.   But although the parents of Caxton little dreamed that the boy who spent his first years running wild over the fields of Kent would one day stand reverenced as the man whose work had brought incalculable benefits to English literature, yet they had a respect for learning and gave the boy all the education that their means would allow.

And we may believe that young Caxton took wise advantage of this, though he had no notion of becoming a great scholar, and can easily imagine him lost to the world around while he bent over some valued manuscript which contained the history of King Arthur, or Helen of Troy, or that prime favorite, Robin Hood, little thinking, as he turned the leaves of the precious volume, that the time would come when he should make it possible for college libraries to unchain their books and pass them freely to all who would read. So little did his parents forecast the future, that when Caxton was eighteen years of age he was considered learned enough for one in his station, and he was therefore apprenticed to one of the wealthiest and most influential

London merchants, Robert Large, to learn his business. The merchants of the fifteenth century were a very important class, and had many other interests beyond those of mere buying and selling. In many cases they owned their own ships, and when these were sent to foreign countries it was the custom for the wealthy and noble classes to commission them to obtain those rare and costly articles which were not then considered regular articles of trade. Thus while the merchants controlled the wool and silk markets, they also bought and sold other wares of an entirely different nature. The master of a ship sailing to the Mediterranean, for example, would be commissioned to bring home with him spices, drugs, ivory, jewelry, and whatever else any patron of the merchant might desire, and among these things it was not unusual to see one or two of those precious manuscripts which were counted of more value than gold or silver.

In this way the young apprentice would still be thrown somewhat in the company of books, and from this time on Caxton found greater and greater delight in such companionship, and thus, from his acquaintance with the popular ballads and poetry which the wandering minstrels made familiar to the country-people in his childhood and by the study of the works of Chaucer and his contemporaries which his life in London enabled him to read, Caxton came to have a very fair knowledge of literature, even before his apprenticeship was over. The apprentices in those days, when merchants and mechanics were all formed into powerful guilds which even the crown treated with great respect, were a not unimportant class. They shared some of the importance of their masters, and were regarded as the inheritors of those privileges which their class had obtained after many weary struggles with the nobility, and in all public festivities they were accorded an honorable share.

Life in those times, when there were such sharp distinctions between the rich and the poor, was not much of a holiday to the working-classes, and their chief amusements were found in those great pageants for which London was then so famous. Whether there had been a great victory won abroad or at home, whether there was a king to be crowned or a royal visitor to receive, or whether the merchants or some other powerful guild wished to display their riches and importance by a public parade, everything was made the occasion for a grand pageant, in which nobles and tradesmen, rich and poor alike, took supreme interest and enjoyment. On these occasions work was entirely given over, and it was to such displays that the apprentice in Caxton's days owed many of his holiday moments; and there can be no doubt that these sights brought their own lessons to the thoughtful lad from Kent, and that many of those grave sayings which came from him later on, and in which he showed such knowledge of the world, may have owed their birth to the thoughts which arose in him in his apprentice days, when he saw such sharp contrasts in life, and could easily read beneath the glitter of the show the feelings which held the hearts of the lookers-on.

This period of Caxton's life was an important one politically, both at home and abroad, and must have made an impress on the mind of the country youth, and perhaps explains the interest which he always took in public affairs. It is certain that life to this apprentice meant much more than the knowledge which bounded his own calling, and it was this susceptibility to other interests which so greatly influenced his later life. It would have been an ordinary matter for the merchant's apprentice to turn merchant himself, send his ships hither and thither and gather for himself riches, and some honor in his calling, and this was doubtless the destiny of more than one youth who shared Caxton's meals in the house of the master. But Caxton could not stop at being a merchant, he must take in other interests, and if any one of these proved greater he must cease being a merchant altogether and follow it wherever it led; such was the character of his mind, and such was his actual experience.

When he was about thirty years of age his old master died, leaving him a sum of money as a mark of his appreciation, and from this time Caxton resided abroad for about twenty years. It is not clearly known why he left London, whether he was deputed on business for his brother-merchants, or whether he chose such a course for his own pleasure. But we do know very well that the principal business that Caxton was about during this time was connected with books and book-making, and that he attained some popularity as a translator and transcriber. At some time during the latter part of his stay abroad Caxton heard of the new art of printing, and from then on never rested until he made the wonderful secret his own. He does not mention in any of the prefaces to the books that he printed, where he learned this art or who was his teacher, and it is probable that he had great difficulty in making the new discovery his own, for whoever held the secret had a prize more valuable than the key to royal treasuries, and it was not easy to persuade one to part with it.

Before the invention of printing, the copying of books had already become a business carried on by others than the monks; and because people who desired books had been in the habit of applying to monasteries which had a reputation for making copies, laymen had come to settle in abbey domains in order to carry on this business more successfully by being near the great depositaries of books as well as near those who desired to buy books. The demand for books was growing and the business of making them was becoming profitable enough to stimulate people's powers of invention to find some way of producing them in large numbers in a short time. Everyone could see that this would be profitable; but no one thought it would so increase the demand for books that the more that were made and the cheaper they could be made the greater the number of books that would be demanded, so that, indeed, larger and larger sums of money would be spent every year for books. And so the inventors of printing, and each man as he learned how to print, endeavored to keep it a secret from everyone else, so as to keep all the profits of the business to himself. At that time a

book made by hand—a manuscript, that is—
cost eight times as much as the first printed
books cost; so it is clear that if the first printers could have prevented others from learning
the business they could have charged as much
as the hand copyists, and so have earned as
much in one year as the copyists earned in
eight. Caxton says that he learned the art of
printing at great expense.

However, he came to this knowledge in good
time, and when he returned to England, somewhere about 1470, and set up his printing-press
there, it was at Westminster that he settled.
For just as the lay copyists settled around
monasteries, so naturally did the first printers.
There is some doubt as to the first book Caxton brought out, both as to its name and the
language in which it was printed; and it is
likely that the very first work from Caxton's
press may not have been the one that gave
him his first fame, but the first book printed in
English by Caxton was the translation of the
Histories of Troy, and it is generally believed
that it was printed at Cologne, where Caxton

probably learned the printer's trade. And then came a time of unceasing work and anxiety, for the setting up of a printing-press was no easy matter. As a rule, all the mechanical part of the work had to be done by the printer himself, assisted only by workmen entirely inexperienced, and often hindered by the enmity of the ignorant; for in those days the unfamiliar was generally considered harmful, and any new art or craft in which machinery was used instead of the labor of men's hands was apt to meet with the hatred and condemnation of the very classes it was calculated to benefit.

The first printing-presses were simply common screw-presses, worked by hand. After the form of types had been inked, and the sheet of paper laid on it, it was run under the screw, which was then brought down upon it. This was very hard work and very slow work, as great care had to be taken that the screw did not come down with too great force and so injure the work, while still sufficient pressure must be used to make a strong impression. The printers made their own ink, and the balls by which it was applied to the types; these balls were made of sheepskin and stuffed with wool, the skins being prepared and the wool carded in the office; and as all these little details were understood only by the master himself, it is easy to imagine the care and anxiety that must have beset Caxton at every step.

After the books were printed they had still, of course, to be bound, and this was also the work of the printer, who had to cover the board sides with leather, silk, or velvet, as the case might require, and ornament them with brass nails, gold, silver, precious stones, or whatever else the fancy of the buyer might dictate. And, last of all, the printer, after his books were printed and bound, had to turn bookseller and sell them himself, though in many cases the selling was done before the book was printed, as it was too great a risk to undertake the expense of printing unless a certain number of subscriptions were obtained beforehand.

Somewhere within the walls of Westminster Abbey, probably in the old scriptorium, Caxton set up the first printing-press in England, and began the great revolution in the art of book-making. As the priests were still the greatest readers, they were the first friends to the new art, and it is undoubtedly owing to the encouragement given it by the religious orders that printing made such comparatively rapid progress from the beginning; for the great mass of people could not even read, and as the cheapness of printing consisted in having as many copies made and sold as possible, it was an easy matter for the old printers to have their stock of books outnumber their readers. Many of the early printers, in all countries, only carried on their art in the midst of the greatest privation and poverty, as the materials were so expensive and the returns so small, and found their only success in the knowledge that they were working for the good of mankind.

And it was this same noble motive which actuated Caxton and which made him do all that he did, not to his own profit, but to the glory of learning and the benefit of his fellow-creatures. This same conscientiousness was carried into every part of his work and is noticed particularly in his translations, many of which he made himself, and in which he always strove to reproduce faithfully the words of the author. This was not an easy matter, as the manuscript copies sometimes differed, and Caxton's greatest grievance in his work was not the fear of pecuniary loss or waste of time, but the thought that perhaps he had not been able, in spite of his care, to give to the reader the exact language of the author.

As was natural in a state of society where reading was a rare accomplishment and the public taste in literature lay in old ballads and romances, many of Caxton's first books were translations from the old tales of chivalry taken either from the French or English romances or from the adventures of Greek and Roman heroes told in the classic poets. These romances had been nearly all introduced into the French by translation, and Caxton's work consisted in putting them into English. His first book, *The Histories of Troy*, being the story of the siege of Troy, was familiar to all the nations of Europe and had delighted the story-loving English people for generations. No book could have been better chosen to invest the new art with charm and win the popular heart, and it was this very way of putting the old romances into English that first turned the English into a nation of readers, and thus accomplished the aim of Caxton much sooner than the publication of religious or philosophical treatises in Latin could possibly have done.

The first book which Caxton printed in England was *The Game and Play of Chess*, which he translated from the French, and which was finished on the last day of March, 1474. This curious old book was much read in those days by kings, bishops, authors, and scholars of every kind, and contained not only a treatise on the origin of the game, but also allusions to law and morals; and, indeed, Caxton's thought in printing it was not so much to popularize the book as to instruct the people in morals. The book takes each piece in the game—king, queen, bishop, knight, rook, and pawn—and deduces from their office, in playing, the duties and obligations of the different classes of society, the eight pawns representing the common people, who were divided into, 1st, tillers of the earth; 2d, workers in metals; 3d, lawyers, scribes, and makers of cloth; 4th, merchants; 5th, physicians; 6th, innkeepers and sellers of provisions; 7th, city guards and receivers of customs; 8th, messengers, couriers, players at dice, and gamblers. And Caxton, in his dedication of the book, said that he hoped that both nobles and common people would find instruction therein and learn to govern themselves as they ought. The second edition of this book is known as the first printed English book which contained wood-cuts to illustrate the text.

Among the first books which followed these two may be mentioned the *Confessio Amantis* of Gower, *The History of Reynard the Fox*, that delightful tale which had charmed Europe for three centuries, *The Fables of Æsop*, *The Life of Jason*, *The Golden Legend*, a compilation of Virgil called *The Book of Eneydos*, *The Poems of Chaucer*, and some well-known books on religion, history, and science, as well as various other works, which bring the number of books printed by our first printer up to sixty-four. Among these old books must be mentioned *The History of King Arthur* and his knights, which first delighted England when introduced by Geoffrey of Monmouth in his *History of Britain*, and which after three hundred years, during which time it had received numerous additions at the hands of various masters, as already related, and had become familiar to Europe, was translated from the French by Sir Thomas Mallory and printed by Caxton in 1485.

From this list it is easily seen that Caxton made his English readers familiar with the best books of all time, and that the Greek and Latin poets, the old philosophers and historians, the mediæval romances and the writings of Chaucer, were put within the reach of all who could read. Caxton's last work was the translation of *The Lives of the Holy Fathers*, which he translated when he was nearly eighty years of age and which he left ready for the press, having finished it on the last day of his life.   His work was carried on by Wynkyn de Worde, his principal assistant, whose devotion to his master and his art made him a worthy sharer in the fame which belongs to the first English printers.

CHAPTER XIII.

EDMUND SPENSER AND THE FAËRY QUEENE.

The early part of the sixteenth century was a time of such stirring adventure and widening of thought that to the practical-minded it must have seemed that the days of elf and fairy had returned. The work of Caxton, begun in such a humble spirit and under the auspices of a few scholars, had spread so far that thousands of books were printed all over England, and the little light which had first burned so unsteadily among the shadows of Westminster was regarded as the guiding-star which would lead to new and wonderful gifts to the race. And before the world had become accustomed to the presence of the printing-press, and still looked upon the invention of Gutenberg as a higher kind of magic, it was called upon to believe in a still greater wonder, which came with such startling force as to overwhelm even the most practical minds and make the unreal seem alone the real.

This was the discovery of America, and the consequent knowledge of the true shape and size of the earth, which at once put aside all the popular fables concerning a flat plane surrounded by impassable seas, and brought to light the presence of another world beyond the Atlantic, as beautiful as the old, peopled with races whose intelligence placed them forever beyond those fabulous creatures which were supposed to inhabit the outer shores of the "sea of darkness," as the ocean was called, and, above all, showed the folly of associating horrors and dangers with the unknown simply because it was unknown.

It was in this regard that the voyage of Columbus did much more than reveal the existence of America and the Western islands, and from this time, instead of shrinking from a knowledge of what lay beyond their own shores, Europeans gladly took advantage of every opportunity to increase their knowledge, and voyages were undertaken, both at public and private expense, for no other object than to visit remote lands, sail through unknown seas, and become familiar with the great countries that Columbus had discovered. The fashion for exploration took such hold on the public mind that the ships could not hold the adventurers who thronged the wharves for a chance to ship to the New World, and the returned navigator was sure of a more interested audience than had ever listened to bard or minstrel, and people found a greater fascination in these true tales than any possessed by story of magic or knightly adventure.

This sudden widening of the physical boundaries of the world seemed to expand men's thoughts in other directions, and suggested to many that what had hitherto seemed impossible might after all be attained. And then there came a time of curious study of all sorts, and alchemy, astrology, and even magic, were pursued with great eagerness in the hope that the unseen world would reveal to the students marvels as unique as those which repaid the toil of

Columbus. All sorts of strange doctrines circulated among the philosophers and mystics and the disciples and believers who followed them, and it was the creed of the hour that time and patience would at last reveal all the mysteries of the universe, and that in some way the knowledge thus gained would prove such a benefit to the race that all the evils which beset mankind would die away and the Golden Age of the old poets once more be possible. Owing to these circumstances it is not strange that the first important book written in English in the sixteenth century should have represented the condition of people's minds at that time; the diaries and records of the great discoverers were fascinating the whole of Europe, and English literature could not fail to be influenced by it. This book was written by Sir Thomas More, a great scholar and one of the foremost men of the day, and describes an imaginary country which the author named Utopia.

This land of fancy, situated in the fairest portion of the globe, had the lofty mountains, magnificent rivers, great forests, beautiful plains,

and agreeable climate which were the charac-
teristics of the New World.   But, more than
this, it was inhabited by a race intellectually and
morally superior to any of the nations known in
history.   The cities in this beautiful land were
marvels of elegance and comfort, and so thoroughly had the Utopians mastered the secret of
government that this beauty was nowhere
dimmed by the squalor and wretchedness of poverty, for in Utopia none were poor.   Each child
was born to a heritage of health, education, and
comfort, and the palaces of the wealthy were
the homes of any who suffered misfortune.   In
this book More embodied all the ideas of a
noble and free government, and sought to portray a state of society in which misery was impossible, because brotherhood was the law of
life ; and it was this which gave the work its
great power and turned it from a mere story of
fancy into a plea for the poorer classes of England, whose condition was hardly more prosperous than in the days when Langlande and Wickliffe had voiced the rebellion of the people,
against the heartless magnificence and cruel in-

difference of the nobility of Edward III. More's book was widely read by all classes of people, who were amused by it although they saw in it only a dream, and it has importance as the first popular book of the sixteenth century in point of time.

But by the middle of the century many of the causes which had interfered with the progress of literature had died away, and England was occupying a position among the nations of Europe higher than any she had ever attained before. The discoveries of English navigators in the New World, the national progress, the presence of some of the greatest statesmen and thinkers in the world, and, above all, the establishment of schools all over the country for the education of the people, placed England so high among European nations that all the faults of government and the selfishness of her monarchs could not detract greatly from her glory.

And it was just at this time, when the wealth of America had begun to pour into the coffers of Europe and men's ideas of the world had undergone a great change, that the next great

English poet after Chaucer came into the world. This was Edmund Spenser, born in 1553, in London, of a noble family, and favored by the circumstances of birth and education to study the condition of English society, while endowed with that sense of justice which would lead him to put such knowledge to good use.

Very little is known of Spenser's early life, but to a keen-eyed and sharp-witted boy the London of his childhood must have been a very interesting place. The talk of the French wars, of the martyrs to the new faith which the Protestants had preached, of the trade and commerce with the New World, and the great schemes of colonization which were spoken of as impracticable dreams, must have been familiar to Spenser in his youth, and there is no doubt that the day-dreams of the adventurers and travellers who were found in every class of society did much to fire the imagination of the boy whose genius was to form one of the chief glories of English literature.

Spenser entered Cambridge when he was sixteen, and in the same year gave evidence of his poetic gifts by publishing some verses in a work which held the contributions of various writers. It was in his college days that he formed some of those friendships which lasted through life, and which somewhat brightened his sad fortunes; and when he left Cambridge, six years after his entrance, he bore with him something of more value than his degree, namely, the interest and affection of those who were to fill high places in later life, and whose greatness of heart well fitted them for the friendship of such an idealist as Spenser.

After leaving college Spenser spent some time in the North of England, returning to London with the manuscripts of several poems, and was introduced by his college friend Gabriel Harvey to Sir Philip Sidney, one of the most gallant courtiers of the day, and a man highly renowned for learning and generosity. This introduction led to an invitation to Penhurst, the beautiful home of Sidney, where all the learned and accomplished men of the times were wont to gather. Here were discussed all the political and intellectual events of the times, and in this congenial society Spenser found the highest inspiration for his literary career.   The poems which he wrote received the warmest praise from Sidney ; and Sidney was considered one of the best of critics, representing in himself the highest culture of the age, and we may well believe that the years which Spenser spent at Penhurst were among the brightest in his life.

Sidney's friendship led in time to Spenser's appointment as secretary to the Lord-Lieutenant of Ireland, a post which he gladly accepted, as it at once relieved him from a position of dependence while it left abundant leisure for his literary pursuits.   He went to Ireland in 1680, and six years afterward he received a grant of land, which led to his looking upon his new possessions as his probable home for the rest of his days.   During all these changes Spenser had been studying the condition of England, its glory and its shame, and forming a plan of a great work which should contain some remedy for those evils which beset his country, and made it, even in that time of power and success, worthy the reproach of many earnest thinkers. Thinking that there is no teacher so powerful as a good example, he resolved to write a poem in which the hero should be a pattern Englishman, possessed of courage, courtesy, honor, and all true manliness, and his story he thought might influence his readers to strive for noble things, and not be content with ignoble aims.

And Spenser thought it wise to put his message to his fellow-men in the form of a fairy tale, for, however men may be occupied, they are always ready to listen to fairy tales. The poem was called *The Faëry Queene*, and this is the story:

Gloriana, Queen of Fairy-land, held every year a feast which occupied twelve days, and to which the whole court was invited. Here were assembled all the great lords and ladies of the kingdom, and the days passed in feasting, merry-making, and all kinds of amusements. At the beginning of one of these feasts there entered into the royal court one morning a young man whose dress and appearance contrasted so strongly with the rest of the company that the magnificently apparelled courtiers looked upon him with surprise. But the new-comer seemed not to notice the humbleness of his dress, and, going up to the Faëry Queene, fell on his knees before her and begged her to grant him the boon of undertaking any knightly task which might be required during the feast. Gloriana and her lords wondered much that such a request should come from one so humble in looks, but she had to grant his wish because such was the law of the feast, though she doubted whether such a person would be able to bring any adventure to a successful and glorious end.

Hardly had this petition been granted when there entered a beautiful maiden, dressed in deep mourning and riding a milk-white ass, followed by a dwarf who carried in one hand a heavy spear and with the other led a noble steed which bore the arms of a knight. This maiden was the Princess Una, whose father and mother had lost their kingdom through the wickedness of a horrible dragon who ravaged

18

the country and then shut the old king and queen up in a brazen tower and kept them there by enchantment. The old king offered his daughter's hand and half his kingdom to any knight who would release him, and Una wandered up and down the earth seeking for a hero to perform this deed. At last she reached the court of Gloriana, and as she entered she fell on her knees before the Queene and begged her assistance.

Then the man whose humble appearance had attracted the wonder of the court came forward, and begged the Queene that the adventure might be his; and because of her promise she was obliged to consent, though she would have preferred some other champion, and Una herself looked with distrust upon the uncouth stranger and told him that the adventure might not be his unless he could wear the armor which she brought, for no one could succeed in the enterprise unless the armor fitted him perfectly. But this did not deter the young man, and everyone was amazed to find that the armor fitted him as if it had been made for him, and gave him such a fine appearance that he seemed the bravest man present. He then received knighthood, and from henceforth was to be known as St. George, the Red-cross Knight, from the red crosses which gleamed on his breast and on his silver shield.

Then he mounted the warlike steed, and, followed by the beautiful maiden and the dwarf, started out on his strange adventure. At first their way led over a pleasant plain, so bright with flowers and fresh with running streams that it made the travellers feel that the whole world must be beautiful; but presently the sky was overcast, the flowers drooped their heads beneath fierce gusts of wind, and Una and her companions were forced to seek shelter from the sudden storm. This they found in a little grove near by, whose thick canopy of leaves hardly allowed the rain to enter, and where the song of the birds, safe in the shady cover, was not interrupted though the storm raged without. This place was so beautiful, with its many kinds of trees and its grassy paths, that the travellers took great delight in wandering through the leafy aisles, not noticing that the paths crossed and recrossed, and twined in and out so as to make a complete labyrinth, until they desired to retrace their steps and pursue their journey. Then they saw that they could find no way out of the wood, for whatever path they took seemed to lead them deeper and deeper in; and, finally, as they were following one which seemed more travelled than the others, they came to a hollow cave, in the midst of dense shadows, and then they stood still in great fear, for they knew not what was before them. But presently the knight gathered courage and entered the dark cave, which was so gloomy that only his armor lightened the thick shadows, and he saw there a fearful beast which rushed angrily at him, and at first so desperate was the struggle that it seemed the knight must be overcome. But at last he gained the victory and left the monster slain at the entrance to the cave, and after this they at last did find a path that led them out of the woods, and went on their journey.

Toward night they met an old man of venerable appearance, clad in the dress of a hermit, who led them to his little lowly hermitage, down in a dale, hard by a forest's side, and begged them to rest there for the night.   They were very glad to accept this invitation, for they were weary with the day's journey ; but they might have much better gone on their way, for the seeming hermit was no other than the wicked Archimago, a powerful magician, all whose days and nights were spent in devising schemes to hurt all who professed goodness, for he was the sworn foe of righteousness and loved only evil.   And no sooner had the knight fallen asleep than Archimago sent to the cave of Morpheus, the God of Sleep, who dwelt in the interior of the earth, and commanded him to send a deceitful dream to the knight which should turn his interest in Una to dislike ; and by means of this dream and other magic Archimago succeeded in his design, and turned the knight's heart against Una, so that he left the cave, taking the dwarf with him, and leaving Una behind him.

And as he went on his way he saw a knight and a lady coming toward him, and the knight bore a great shield with the legend *Sans foy*—without faith—written upon it, and the lady was clothed in a scarlet robe, trimmed with gold and pearls, and wore on her head a crown of jewels, and rode a palfrey whose trappings were of costly design and whose bridle " rung with golden bells and bosses brave." Sansfoy rushed to meet St. George and challenged him to combat, and after a fearful struggle the Redcross Knight conquered his foe, and took under his protection the lady, who told him that she was the daughter of a great emperor and that Sansfoy had carried her off without her permission and kept her a captive. The two journeyed on together until the heat of noon drove them to take shelter beneath two wide-spreading trees, and as they were resting in the shade the knight plucked a bough from the tree to twine a garland for the lady's forehead.

But as he did so he was horrified to find the wounded tree dropping blood, and heard a piercing shriek, and then a voice told him that the two trees were two hapless lovers who had been transformed by the magic of the great enchantress Duessa, and warned the knight to beware of the cruel witch who had wrought them this woe. And when the knight turned to look at his companion he found her in a swoon, for she herself was the false Duessa, and she feared that the knight might suspect her. But he did not doubt her, and, raising her up from the ground put her on her palfrey, and they went on their way, the knight still thinking her the fairest lady he had ever seen.

In the meantime the unfortunate Una had been wandering everywhere in search of the knight, not knowing why he had left her and fearful that some disaster had happened him. And on the second day, being very weary, she alighted and lay down to rest in a quiet wood, which was so full of shadows that her own face made all the sunshine in it ; and as she lay there, weary with her journey and with her heart full of fear, a savage lion rushed suddenly from the wood, greedy for the prey which he saw before him. But as he came nearer the sight of Una's pure and lovely face tamed his savage heart, and instead of doing her harm he came and fawned at her feet and licked her hands, and when she arose to go he would not leave her, but followed her on her journey, the loyalest champion she could have had, guarding her while she slept, and when she woke reading her will from her eyes and performing it with faithful service.

And as Una went on seeking her knight, through all the ways that she thought he might have passed, her eyes were at last gladdened by the sight of a noble-looking knight whose shield gleamed brightly beneath the well-remembered red cross, and as he came nearer she saw the features she had been seeking so long. It was not her knight, however, but the magician Archimago, who had taken on the knight's likeness by witchcraft, hoping by this means to lead Una away from her search and keep her separated from her true knight. But Una thought it was St. George, and the two journeyed on together until they met Sansloy, a brother of Sansfoy whom St. George had slain, and who challenged Archimago to battle. In this encounter the old magician was unhorsed, and his disguise discovered, and Una had hardly time to recover from this shock before Sansloy seized her as his captive, and, when the brave lion came to the rescue, killed the noble beast with his sword and so left Una quite unprotected.

Her shrieks for help brought out from a neighboring forest a number of the satyrs, fauns, and nymphs who lived there, and these kindly wood-gods drove away Sansloy and took the maiden to their own sylvan home, where she lived peacefully for a long time, teaching her rude friends the arts and customs of civilization, and regarded by all as an honored guest. In the meantime St. George had had many strange adventures, and had at last been taken captive by a cruel giant and confined in a dungeon, and the dwarf, who had followed him all along, seeing that he could be of no service in this new trouble, left him and fled, in the hope of meeting the Lady Una.   And in this he was successful, for Una had left the home of the wood-gods under the protection of a kindly satyr, and begun anew her search for the Red-cross Knight.

The dwarf told her of his misfortunes, and they wandered through forests and over hills and through many a valley, and just when their hearts were despairing they met a noble knight whose majestic appearance at once commanded their respect, and to him Una told her sad story. This knight was no other than the great Prince Arthur himself, whose golden helmet, infolded with the shining wings of the famous dragon, flashed a brightness all around, and whose shield was made not of brass or steel, but of one great diamond no human blade could pierce. Arthur at once promised to go to the relief of St. George, and they came at last to the giant's castle; and the Red-cross Knight was once more able to see the light of day, and Una bore him away with her to a palace where dwelt the three sisters, Faith, Hope, and Charity, and here the knight was cured of his wounds.

And when he was once more able to travel, the knight and Una went on again, and came at last to her own country. And then she showed him the brazen tower in which her parents were confined, and they saw the watchman pacing the walls, and looking far over the plain to see if any friend might be in sight; for Una had been gone so long that her parents were in despair and feared that even this last retreat would be taken from them if help did not soon arrive. And as the knight and Una stood look· ing at the tower they heard a dreadful roaring which filled the air, and then they espied the dragon, stretched along the side of a hill, his scaly form glittering in the sun, and his eyes gleaming with the horrid light of hate, and in a few moments he spread his wings and came swiftly toward them, and St. George had hardly placed Una in a safe spot before he was at his side awaiting the combat.

The Red-cross Knight and the dragon fought all day, and neither could claim the victory, though both were sorely wounded, and when night came the end seemed near, for with a dreadful stroke the dragon felled his opponent to the ground, and Una thought that he was slain. But as St. George fell under the dragon's charge he found himself lying in the waters of a magic well which possessed healing virtues, and in the morning he was again ready for the combat. And again they fought all day, and again the dragon gave St. George a deadly stroke which deprived him of all strength, and this time he found himself beside a fair tree from which flowed a stream of healing balm, and the dragon dared not approach it because of its sacred nature—and so the knight rested there, and in the morning his wounds were healed again.

With the first break of day the fight began again, and then it seemed that St. George had only gained strength in the preceding conflicts, for he beset the dragon so vigorously and courageously that the monster thought it best to end the fray at once, and, opening his horrid jaws, advanced toward the Red-cross Knight, intending to swallow him. But St. George only took advantage of this manner of attack to thrust his faithful sword into the dragon's mouth with such might that the life-blood came rushing out in deadly streams, and, sinking back, the monster soon breathed his last. Then the watcher on the brazen tower called down the joyful news to his lord and lady, and the old king came forth and looked at his dead enemy and knew that his trials were over at last.

Then the brazen gates were opened wide, and the trumpets sounded from the towers, proclaiming joy and peace to all the land, and all the prisoners were set free, and the liberated soldiery followed the king and queen in grave procession, carrying laurels in their hands, and accompanied by maidens bearing garlands of flowers, and they all knelt before the Red-cross Knight and did homage to him as their deliverer. And then began a time of feasting and merrymaking, which ended with the betrothal of Una and her brave knight ; and so the story ends.

This is the first book of the Faëry Queene, and by it Spenser meant to give to the world an allegory which should teach men to be faithful to their trust and live righteously. The

Red-cross Knight signifies Holiness, and Una signifies snow-white Truth; the trials and final victories of the knight typifying the struggles of the human soul after righteousness. Spenser intended to have twelve books in the poem, each book to portray the adventures of some knight who typified one of the moral virtues. But this design was never carried out, as only six of the twelve books were ever written. The five others which were finished represent Temperance, Purity, Friendship, Justice, and Courtesy, and in each book Prince Arthur comes in as the great helper to the hero, it being the purpose of Spenser to represent the great English favorite Arthur as typifying the sum of all the virtues, since the hero of each book depends on him for aid.

In the second book the hero is Sir Guyon, who has been appointed by the Faëry Queene to destroy a wicked enchantress named Acrasia. He left the court accompanied by his trusty palmer, and as they were passing by a deep forest they heard a piercing shriek. This cry of distress appealed to Sir Guyon, who was a true knight, and he entered the forest hastily to see who might need his help. And there he found a little babe by the side of its dying mother, while near by lay the dead body of a brave knight. The mother told Sir Guyon that her husband had been made a prisoner by the magic of Acrasia, and had met his death through her enchantments, while she herself was dying from her despair at his loss. This tale touched Sir Guyon's heart, and he promised the mother that he would care for her child and wreak vengeance on Acrasia, and he watched her faithfully till she breathed her last, and then buried her and her husband, and swore by their grave that he would never rest till he had avenged their wrong.

Then he took the child up gently and tried in vain to wash away the blood-stains on its little hands; but this could not be done because of enchantment, so he was obliged to leave them still bloody, for the water was charmed and could not be stained by anything that touched it. So Sir Guyon returned to the road where he had left his steed, but found that it had disappeared, and, still carrying the babe, he proceeded on his way on foot, and came before long to a castle, where he had a battle with two faithless knights, whom he subdued, and where he left the babe in the care of one of the ladies of the castle, who promised to bring him up with all tenderness and care. As he went on his way he met with many strange adventures while trying to find the Idle Lake, in the midst of which, on a little island, dwelt the enchantress Acrasia.

And in his journey he also met with many temptations. Once he was taken down to the centre of the earth where dwelt the god Mammon, in a house hewn out of the rock, and whose walls and roof and floor were covered with gold and gems, and where there were chests filled with such wealth as Sir Guyon had never dreamed of, and all this Mammon offered him if he would leave his quest and serve him ; but he would not, and after three days of temptation he returned to the upper air again, but could go no farther on his way that day, for he

was weak and faint from his trial and fell into a
deadly swoon as soon as the outer air touched
his forehead. And there the faithful palmer
found him and tried to resuscitate him, but
while he was thus engaged two of Sir Guyon's old enemies appeared and attempted
to rob him of his armor, thinking that he
was dead. Just then Prince Arthur appeared,
and after a great battle with the knights subdued them just as Sir Guyon awoke from his
trance.

And then, after a visit to the Castle of Temperance, Sir Guyon embarked once more on
the waters of the Idle Lake, and passed by
the Gulf of Greediness, which swallowed up all
boats that came near it, and the Magnetic Rock,
which drew ships to its shores only to dash
them to pieces, and saw afar off the Wandering Islands, on which whoever stepped should
never return, but wander forevermore as the
islands themselves. And they passed also
through rolling waves wherein swam hydras
and sea-satyrs and other dreadful monsters of
the deep; and the Bay of Mermaids, whose

19

dwellers sang sweet songs to them and tried to woo them from their purpose; and when they were past that, innumerable monster birds came flying from the upper air and surrounded the boat and uttered harsh screams to frighten the travellers away.

But they held to their purpose, and at last reached the enchanted island and landed safely, and when they found themselves attacked by the savage beasts that wandered on the shores they still passed on undisturbed, for the palmer's magic wand turned these ravenous monsters once more into human shape and freed them from the enchantment of Acrasia. And then passing through a beautiful garden, they came to the bower where Acrasia dwelt, and Sir Guyon bound Acrasia in chains of adamant and destroyed the groves and bowers and palace, and left the place desolate, so that it should never more tempt anyone to ruin. And then Sir Guyon departed, having achieved his adventure gloriously, as became such a noble knight; and thus ends the second book.

In the third book we have the story of the beautiful heroine Britomart:

Britomart was the daughter of the King of Wales, for whom Merlin, the enchanter, had made a magic mirror in which could be seen all things that were happening afar off and all things that should happen in the future. And this mirror was considered the glory and honor of Wales and its chief defence, as no foe could ever attack the kingdom unawares, because the king could always see the approach of the enemy in his mirror, long before the borders of his country were reached, and when the foe came they were met by such a force that they were content to fly without offering battle. One day Britomart went up to the magic mirror, and, looking in out of vain curiosity, saw in the distance the vision of an armed knight, wearing armor of antique design which was adorned with gold and had engraved on it the legend—*Achilles's arms which Artegal did win.* On the crest of his helmet was a hound *couchant,* and on his shield a crowned ermelin which showed white against the azure field. And as Britomart looked on the knight and saw his noble features and manly bearing, her heart went out to him, and she felt that here was the knight who might win her hand and rule the Kingdom of Wales when her father had passed away.

But no one at the court had even heard of a knight by the name of Artegal, and Britomart was in despair, and began to wonder if she should ever meet him, after all; and under this despair she pined away until Glaucé, her old nurse, was alarmed, and gathered all sorts of herbs and made tea for her to drink, and wove all sorts of charms, and tried in every way to undo the spell, but could not. Then she took her to Merlin's cave and begged him to give his advice, and Merlin said that Britomart would surely wed Artegal at last, though she should pass through many strange adventures before that time came, and said that she must go forth in search of him and bring him back with her to Wales. And so Britomart dressed herself in the armor of a beautiful queen that her father had once captured, and, taking the magic spear, stole forth from her father's court and started on her quest, accompanied by Glaucé, who was disguised as a squire, and did not rest until she came to Fairy Land.

And while she was journeying she met Sir Guyon and Prince Arthur, who had been wandering up and down after adventures ever since they left the Idle Lake, and Sir Guyon, thinking that Britomart was a man, engaged in battle with her, but was speedily disarmed because of the magic spear.   Then, as each one admired the other's bravery, they swore friendship and went on their way together; but they soon parted company, for Sir Guyon and the Prince left her in order to rescue the beautiful Florimel, who was pursued by an enemy, and Britomart went on alone.   And presently she came to a fine castle, pleasantly situated between a forest and a plain, and she saw on the plain six knights striving against one.   This aroused her indignation and she pushed forward to help the one who was at such disadvantage, and with her magic spear soon disarmed three of the knights, and the others yielded, and invited the two strangers into the castle. The strange knight whom Britomart rescued was St. George, who was on a new adventure, and to him Britomart confided her secret and found out that the Red-cross Knight knew Artegal very well, and that he was as brave a knight as maiden ever loved; and when the new friends had to separate, Britomart went on her way cheered by the thought that the knight she was seeking was so worthy.

In the meantime Artegal himself was wandering through Fairy Land on a certain quest, and, although Britomart did not know it, they were coming nearer every day.

Artegal when a child had been under the care of Astræa, the goddess who taught mankind the laws of justice, and whose wise instruction had made Artegal one of the greatest knights in Fairy Land. She had first been attracted to him while seeing him at play with his little companions, for his face was full of noble purpose even in childhood; and so with gifts and winning words she induced him to go with her to the cave where she dwelt, and for many years he lived there, learning useful things. And when his education was finished Astræa gave him the sword Chrysaor, the most perfect sword in the world, garnished with gold, and of such temper that it could cleave any armor. And she gave him as his companion the sturdy Talus, who carried an iron brand, and was often called the Lion-man; and the first adventure that Gloriana gave him was to destroy the tyrant Grandtorto, who had taken away the Lady Irena's heritage, and kept it while the distressed princess had fled to the court for relief.

And Artegal and Britomart had many strange adventures before they met; but they both came at last to a great tournament that was being held for the prize of a golden girdle. Here were all the most famous knights in Fairy Land, who all did such wondrous deeds that the tournament was famed forever after. Here came Artegal, clad in uncouth armor, and created a great sensation by his looks, for no one knew him because of his disguise; and, brilliant as were the other achievements of the festival, they all paled before the exploits of

Artegal, who would surely have carried off the prize had he not been challenged in the moment of victory by another knight who had just entered the lists. This knight unhorsed first Artegal and then many other knights, and claimed the victory; and it was no wonder that success followed him, for it was no other than Britomart, whose magic spear no one could withstand. Artegal went on his way after the tournament, and Britomart went on hers, not knowing that she had met her hero; but they met again afterward as they were following their separate quests and Artegal challenged Britomart to combat.

The struggle was so furious that Britomart had hard work to keep her courage, even with her magic spear, and it was only when a hard stroke from Artegal tore away part of her helmet, revealing the beauty of her face, that her opponent showed signs of yielding; for some secret power led Artegal to think that it would bring woe and sorrow to him if he harmed such glorious beauty, and he begged her to discontinue the fight. But she would not, and stood over him ready to strike, when he raised his visor and disclosed the features of the hero she had been seeking. The shock deprived her of all strength, when she found that it was really Artegal and no other, but Glaucé soon made matters straight by telling Artegal of Britomart's vision, and the two were soon after betrothed.

But Artegal had still to perform his quest of destroying Grandtorto, and was obliged to leave Britomart for the time, promising to return to her in three months. This mission Artegal was able to accomplish, but not singly, for Britomart herself went to his assistance finally, and also Prince Arthur, and at last the tyrant was subdued and Artegal free of his duty to Gloriana.

The story of Britomart and Artegal, with many other incidents thrown in, occupies the third, fourth, and fifth books of *The Faëry Queene*, and shows the triumph of Purity, Friendship, and Justice. Besides *The Faëry Queene*, Spenser wrote many other beautiful poems, some of them before and some of them during the time that he was composing his great poem. Among these may be mentioned *The Shepherd's Calendar*, a collection of twelve poems, each celebrating one month of the year, and which was one of his earliest poems, the *Epithalamion*, a song in honor of his own marriage, considered the most beautiful of all marriage-songs; some hymns in honor of Love and Beauty, many beautiful sonnets, and various other poems. Of these minor poems the most beautiful of all is that called *Astrophel*, which is a lament for the death of Sir Philip Sidney—the poet's warm friend, and the most perfect flower of English knighthood.

Spenser died in 1599 in London, whither he had returned from Ireland after the destruction of his house by a mob. At his own request he was buried in Westminster, near Chaucer. He is sometimes called the " poets' poet," because his works are more cared for by poets than by the general reader. He has been the inspiration of some of the greatest writers in English literature, and the greatest poets of succeeding ages have delighted in calling him master.

CHAPTER XIV.

Spenser's friend and admirer, Sir Philip Sidney, whose fame as a courtier, knight, and gentleman, filled all Europe, and who was the brightest ornament of Elizabeth's court, was himself a writer of no mean merit even in those days of literary power, and both from their connection with the literary history of the times and the character of their author, his writings will always find an honored place in English literature.

Sidney was born on the 29th of November, 1554, at beautiful Penshurst Castle in Kent, which had been in possession of the family for many years. The Sidneys were of honorable lineage and had been intimately connected with the nobility of England both by their marriage and descent, and, indeed, as the mother of Sir Philip was the great-granddaughter of Henry VII., he was on that side a descendant of the very monarch who laid the foundations of England's greatness after the devastating period of the Wars of the Roses. As a mark of favor to the Sidney family, Queen Mary, who was then upon the throne, made him the namesake of her husband, Philip II. of Spain, a circumstance of itself sufficient to show the standing of the family and their importance at court, though more than one member had before this felt the weight of royal displeasure.

At Penshurst the birthday of the young heir was marked by the planting of an acorn, the oak from which grew to a mighty tree and held its own for more than two centuries after the hands that planted it had been dust. In this beautiful home, and under the care of his gifted father and mother, Sidney passed his early youth, amid such surroundings as were well calculated to fit him for the life he was to follow, both nature and circumstances combining to make the training of the youth who was to become the perfect pattern of English chivalry as complete as possible.

Sidney was destined by his father to be a courtier and statesman, and every part of his education was most carefully attended to. All the accomplishments of the day—music, fencing, dancing, the art of graceful talk and gay compliment, of perfect dressing and courtly manner —were as much a part of his training as the Greek and Latin and science which attracted his mind so greatly, and which had such a charm for him that he would have been well content to forego the tediousness of court-life and give all his heart to learning had this seemed his greatest duty. But Sidney lived in times when the greatest men were men of action, and when personal courage and keen foresight were reckoned of greater service to the State than deep learning. English navigators and explorers were busy in the Western world and up among the Arctic seas, trying to add to England's greatness by discovery and claim. English statesmen were busy at foreign courts making policies that insured England's proud position among the other nations of Europe, and everywhere action seemed to be the word of the hour. Some of the greatest navigators, statesmen, and generals were men who had won their fame early in life, and Sidney's first impulse and earliest ambition after he had left boyhood was to distinguish himself early in some useful career.

After his college life was over he passed two years in travel, visiting different courts and learning all that he could of practical statesmanship from the exciting events which were making the history of those days ; and it was while he was on this tour that he first noticed the condition of Europe as a whole, and was able to compare the policy of one country with that of another, and to reason out the causes that led to comfort in one place and distress in another, and thus learn those lessons of political economy which are so necessary to the statesman. Nothing that he saw was uninteresting to Sidney. Whether it was a gay pageant in Venice, a grave session of lords at the German court, or an assemblage of those artists, musicians, and poets who graced the French and Italian cities, each seemed equally important and worth finding a lesson in ; and chief among these lessons was the terrible one taught by the St. Bartholomew massacre, when for seven days France ran red with the blood of thousands of Protestants.

Sidney, with other of his countrymen, found refuge at this time at the house of the English Ambassador, and, as the fearful slaughter went on around him, he had ample time to study the awful effect of an intolerance in religion which taught no pity for young or old outside of its own faith. Perhaps even then he had some premonition of the time when duty would call him to help stem the tide of a vengeance as pitiless and murderous as that of St. Bartholomew. After his return to England he was presented to Elizabeth by his uncle, the Earl of Leicester, the most powerful nobleman of the time and the chief favorite of the Queen, and from this time his life was intimately connected with the history of England at that time. He was considered the most promising and brilliant of Elizabeth's courtiers, but the English people learned to love him for that manliness and nobility of character which made him the idol of the nation, and gave him a fame that is still undimmed after three hundred years.

Honor, glory, truth, loyalty, and all virtue seemed to his countrymen to embody themselves in Sir Philip Sidney, and there is no greater tribute to his popularity than the fact that he was thus ideally loved although a near relation and under the patronage of the unscrupulous and unpopular Earl of Leicester. In the midst of this life of action and excitement Sidney found time to devote himself somewhat to literature, and after a period of service at court, during which he thought of himself only as a statesman studying the best interests of England, or after one of those long festivals which Elizabeth delighted in, when days and weeks were given to masques, balls, tournaments, and gayeties of every description, and in which he was required to take a prominent part, because Elizabeth would never dispense with the service of the handsome and knightly young courtiers who surrounded her, he would retire to Penshurst Castle and give his mind to the writing of poetry or romance, finding in this world of fancy the rest which his brain and heart demanded.

At such times he loved to gather around him all the poets and scholars of the day, finding his truest pleasure in their interests and pursuits, and proving by his own compositions that he was worthy of his own place in their company. Here he wrote sonnets and love-poems, some of which are considered beautiful yet, though marred by the excessive use of sentiment which characterized the age; and here, to please his sister, he wrote the famous romance *Arcadia.* In this story he imagines a world remote from the exciting scenes of the court-life with which he was familiar, and peopled by a race whose simple lives and humble ambitions made them fit dwellers in that ideal region which had been the theme of many a poet and romancer. This is the story:

There was once a country which was famed all over the world for its beauty and the happiness of its people, and which enjoyed every gift which it was possible for nature to bestow. The hills were crowned with stately trees, the valleys were bright with silver streams, the meadows were spangled with fair flowers, and every verdant pasture was well stored with the sheep which formed the chief wealth of the country. The peaceful groves were never disturbed by ruder sounds than the songs of birds, and every hill-side and plain echoed to the music of the shepherd's fife; and a thought of this country suggested only fair days and starlit nights, and the charm of sweet melodies. The life of the people was but a succession of happy days, and the shepherds and shepherdesses of Arcadia were often envied by those whom fortune had placed in high positions; and many a courtier and prince and noble lady, tired with the wearisome magnificence of court-life, longed to leave it far behind them, and slip away to Arcadia and turn shepherd or shepherdess, and spend their days by the margins of pleasant streams, in the company of the birds and flowers.

Even the greatest king was considered less a subject for envy than an Arcadian shepherd, and the character of this country and its people so impressed itself upon all surrounding nations that the word Arcadia came to stand for peace and quiet content, and a life of unending happiness. Here lived King Basilius and his wife Gynecia, in serene comfort, until one day word reached the court that a celebrated oracle had declared that grief and woe would come upon the king and all his people from the marriage of his daughters. Overwhelmed by these tidings, the king resolved to hide himself and family in the trackless depths of the forest, and so avert the disaster by keeping his daughters unmarried, and he passed many years undisturbed in this retirement.

But one day, as two shepherds of a neighboring country were lying on a sandy beach, discussing the beauty of a certain shepherdess, they saw the fragment of a wreck approaching, to which clung a man, almost insensible from suffering and exposure. The shepherds rescued and restored him, and as soon as he could speak he begged them to seek for his friend, who was also on the wrecked vessel. The stranger, whose name was Musidorus, was a prince from a distant court, and his friend Pyrocles, whose loss he mourned, was also a prince; and as Musidorus had saved from the wreck a casket of valuable jewels, he promised to reward them well if they would search for his friend. Some fishermen were easily engaged to undertake this mission, and hardly had the search begun when they saw approaching, seated upon a broken mast, Pyrocles himself, whose wondrous beauty and garments of silk and gold led the fishermen to think him some god of the sea. But Musidorus had hardly explained that it was really his friend before a pirate ship hove in sight on a cruise for slaves for the galleys, and the fishermen in terror rowed hastily back to land, leaving Pyrocles to his fate.

Musidorus was in despair at this calamity, and only found comfort when the shepherds advised him to seek the help of Kalander, an Arcadian renowned for his kindness and compassion; and then they led him to Arcadia, which was celebrated for its hospitality and whose people knew of no greater pleasure than to entertain strangers with the music and dancing and games which were their chief enjoyment. They arrived at Kalander's house and were received with the greatest courtesy and kindness, and after Musidorus's story was told, Kalander lost no time in sending out a galley in search for Pyrocles, of whom, however, no tidings could be heard.

While a guest in the house of Kalander, Musidorus noticed the pictures of Basilius, Gynecia, and their daughters, and, on asking who they were, Kalander told him of the oracle's prophecy, and how the royal family were in retreat in the forest. This story at once interested Musidorus, who was much fascinated by the beauty of the royal princesses; but before he had time to dwell upon it very long, word was brought to Kalander that his son Clitophon had been taken prisoner in a distant country, and Musidorus joined the Arcadians in attempting a rescue. After a battle with the enemy, Musidorus proposed to decide the victory by a single combat with the captain of the foe, for the Arcadians were losing ground and Musidorus feared their defeat, and was sure that he could vanquish any single man. This plan was agreed to, and a skilful fight ensued, during which Musidorus received a blow which knocked off his helmet, and immediately afterward was astonished to see his opponent kneel at his feet and offer his sword. But astonishment soon turned to joy when he discovered that he had been fighting with his lost friend Pyrocles, and, as this discovery led to a reconciliation, Clitophon was released and the Arcadians returned home.

And now, when all seemed well again, Pyrocles suddenly fell into deep melancholy and took advantage, when they were out on a hunt, to flee from Arcadia, leaving a letter behind him telling Musidorus that he was hopelessly in love and that he could only find comfort in solitude. Musidorus sought him far and near unsuccessfully, and one day, while resting under the shade of a tree, he was surprised by the sight of his friend, disguised as an Amazon, wearing a doublet of blue satin covered with gold plates in imitation of mail, and carrying at his side a sword. Pyrocles then confessed that he had fallen in love with the portrait of Philoclea, Basilius' daughter, which hung in Kalander's house, and, in despair of ever seeing her, had taken this disguise, sought the retreat of Basilius, and represented himself as a shipwrecked Amazonian Queen. He was well received by Basilius, and no inducement could make him return to Kalander's house. Therefore Musidorus returned with him to the king's house and was introduced as an Arcadian shepherd, and immediately fell in love with Pamela, the other daughter. The two friends then told the sisters their story and were rejoiced to find that their affection was returned, and only the fear of Basilius in regard to the prophecy kept them from revealing their identity to the king.

But now came a new trouble. Amphialus, Prince of Argus and nephew to King Basilius, sought the hand of Philoclea in marriage; and when this was refused his mother sent a party of armed men to Arcadia who seized the two princesses and Pyrocles, while they were wandering through the forest, and bore them to Argus and shut them up in a strong castle built on a lofty rock in the midst of a lake. And here the captives had a hard time of it, for Queen Cecropia made use of every device she could think of to persuade either Philoclea or Pamela to marry her son. But neither bribes nor threats could induce the princesses to be untrue to their lovers, and even the prospect of death but made them all the firmer in their determination.

Basilius in vain attacked the fortress, and Cecropia was exultant in the hope of victory when news was brought that turned her joy to fear. The news of the capture of the sisters had spread through Greece, and everywhere brave and renowned warriors grew angry at the thought of such tyranny, and hastened with offers of assistance to Basilius. And then followed a siege whose length and fierceness were unprecedented in the annals of Arcadia, and during which Cecropia used all her wits to bring the sisters to her wishes. They suffered the most barbarous treatment, and Cecropia, by an ingenious artifice, made each one believe that the other had been beheaded before her eyes. But when this was discovered by Amphialus, who was at heart a gentle prince and only followed his mother's advice in retaining the princesses, he was so incensed that his mother, fearing he meant to kill her, threw herself from the castle roof, and was killed. Amphialus, in his horror, immediately fell upon his sword and died, and thus the castle fell into the hands of Basilius. After a few minor misfortunes the lovers were united at last; and thus ends the romance of *Arcadia*.

The story was read by every courtier and lady of Elizabeth's court, and not only delighted England but was translated into several languages, and continued to be the favorite romance of England for many a year; though the author, when it was finished, expressed the fear that, like the spider's web, it would be thought only fit to be swept away. Perhaps the charm of this story, in which shepherds and shepherdesses and scenes of rural beauty form the chief interest, may have been all the greater in those times when the court of Elizabeth was so often the scene of those magnificent pageants in which she delighted, and which recalled the days of myth, or the more modern amusements of chivalry.

On one of these occasions Sidney himself wrote a play in which shepherds and shepherdesses descanted on love, and where foresters and farmers talked eloquently on the same subject. This play or masque was written at the request of Sidney's uncle, the Earl of Leicester, whom Queen Elizabeth sometimes visited, and whose delight it was to crowd the days and nights with tournaments, masques, and amusements of every kind. At these entertainments the revellers turned themselves into fauns, satyrs, naiads, nymphs, mermaids, and Greek goddesses, while the castle was flooded with music, and representations of the classic myths gave reality to the scene.

But amid these brilliant festivities, in which Sidney often took part, he lost none of that seriousness of purpose which was his chief characteristic, and he stood ready at any moment to serve his country in the highest sense of the word. And in due time his opportunity came. The Netherlands had been trying for many years to rid themselves of the tyranny of Philip II. of Spain, to whom these countries had come as part of his inheritance, and had more than once applied to England for aid. The chief grievance of the people was the refusal of Philip to allow them religious freedom, and the war which lasted so long was a religious war.

Philip II. was the chief representative of the Catholic power in Europe, and declared openly that he would rather see every inhabitant of the country burned alive than have the Netherlands become Protestant. Thousands of people perished under the Inquisition for refusing to renounce their faith, and thousands more perished simply because they were suspected of sympathy with the Protestants. Queen Elizabeth was naturally the hope of the Netherlands in those dark days, for England was Protestant, and was considered of sufficient importance to check the power of Spain if she so willed. But for a long time Elizabeth did nothing but profess sympathy and made no offer of help, though the horrors of the Inquisition grew blacker every year.

At last, however, after the death of William of Orange, the leader of the revolted provinces and their chief support, and just when their fortunes seemed darkest, Elizabeth agreed to furnish the Netherlands with soldiers to help carry on the war; and among the leaders selected to take charge of the fortresses commanding the entrance to the country was Sir Philip Sidney, who was appointed Governor of Flushing. Heartened by the help of the English, the Dutch continued their brave resistance, and the power of Philip was held in check for another year.

In the autumn of 1586 the English laid siege to Zutphen, encamping around the city in the hope that there would be a speedy surrender, for the garrison was weak and the town but poorly supplied with provisions. But the Spaniards had no intention of allowing the surrender of this important point, and the Duke of Parma, commanding Philip's forces, at once marched to the relief of the city. In the morning of a late September day, while city and camp lay shrouded in the white mist which had crept up from the river, the two armies met, and there followed a battle so fierce and bloody that the day became memorable even in that time of horror when victory was often purchased only by slaughter, and it was the boast of the Spaniards to leave not a single human being alive in the cities that they captured. The English fought with such valor and fearlessness that the Spaniards thought they must be under the protection of the powers of evil, for all the flower of the Spanish and Italian cavalry were in the field, which was held by the English in spite of the furious charges of their enemy.

In the presence of the bravest knights and generals, not only of England but of all Europe, Sidney performed such acts of bravery and heroism as to well sustain his reputation as the finest knight in England, and even the enemy were forced to admire his fearless enthusiasm.

Wherever the danger seemed greatest, or a friend appeared surrounded by enemies, the white war-horse of Sidney would be seen dashing through the ranks of his foes; and more than once the fortunes of the battle turned favorably to the English because of his presence at a critical moment. And perhaps, if it had been left to him to choose the manner of his death, he would have been well pleased with the fate that befell him on the field of Zutphen, for it was while he was trying to rescue one of his friends who seemed surrounded by overpowering numbers that Sidney himself received his death-wound and fell fighting for his friend.

His hurt was so severe that he was borne at once from the field, and his last act, as he left the scene of hate and carnage, was in keeping with the whole of his noble life; he had asked for water, a luxury hard to obtain in that hour, and as he was about to raise the cup to his lips he saw the eyes of a dying soldier fixed longingly upon it. "Thy necessity is greater than mine," said Sidney, in answer to that mute appeal, and, without tasting the refreshing draught, he handed the cup to his suffering comrade, thus showing to the end his generous and chivalric spirit, and with his last strength redeeming the horrors of the field of Zutphen by an act which shone like a star through the gloom of that fateful day, and which will be remembered as long as men love, and die for, justice and humanity.

Sixteen days afterward, on October 17, 1586, he breathed his last, while listening to the music he had called for a short time before. England mourned Sidney as her pride and joy, and Elizabeth honored his memory with a funeral whose magnificence was royal in character. His body was carried to England in a ship whose sails and tackling were of black, and which was accompanied with several other ships bearing the highest personages as a guard. The ceremonies in London, where all the nobility and higher classes appeared in mourning, were of the most imposing nature. He was buried in St. Paul's Cathedral, and the poets and scholars of the day vied with one another in writing an epitaph which should fully express the love and gratitude of the nation.　But Sidney's best memorial was written in the hearts of the English people, who beheld in him the ideal of every virtue, and who cherished his untarnished fame as one of their most glorious possessions.

CHAPTER XV.

Among other great literary events which distinguished the sixteenth century and made it the most remarkable in the history of English literature, must be counted the development of the drama.

But although the art of writing plays reached its greatest height during this period, its beginnings were very humble, and were due to the wants and amusements of the people at a time far distant from the days of Elizabeth.

Like the poetry of Cædmon, the English drama had its origin in religious feeling, and dates back to the time when the great body of the nation was still almost entirely ignorant of books, and depended upon the popular traditions, romances, and stories for all interests outside their daily life.

21

And as the people were taught by these stories to honor courage, knighthood, and loyalty, the priests tried in the same way to teach the doctrines of Christianity by bringing them forward in a way that would interest the people and hold their attention.

The stories of the Bible and the legends of the saints were familiar to the people only through the pictures which were painted on the walls of the churches, and the stories which they heard from the lips of the priests or other religious instructors.

The Bible was written only in Greek or Latin, and could be read only by the learned; and although it might have been put into the language of the people as easily as any other book, the priests did not think this, for it was one of their most cherished beliefs that the ignorant could not be made to understand the great mysteries taught by the Church, and that the Bible in the hands of the peasant could only do him harm.

For this reason, when it seemed desirable to teach the people more of Bible or Church history than could be taught by pictures, or in sermons, a custom arose of presenting scenes of a religious nature in the form of plays; and these plays, written by monks and acted by priests and students from the schools, were the beginnings of the English drama.

When such a play dealt with the life of a saint it was called a *Miracle Play*—when it had for its subject the Bible-stories it was called a *Mystery*.

These plays were given on religious festivals, or on any anniversary of importance; the stage was built within the cathedral, and the play was a part of the service for the day, and was generally given during the time which would have been occupied by the reading of the Lesson.

In these plays the stage was generally divided into three platforms, one above the other, representing Heaven, Earth, and Hell, and holding the angels, human beings, and fiends, who were supposed to take part in the performance. The costumes of the actors were as magnificent as could be obtained, it being thought no harm to use the priests' vestments when the priests themselves were the actors, and all the ornaments and service of the church were considered available for the purposes of the play.

Sometimes these plays were very long, and often occupied a week in the performance. Great pains were taken to make the scenes and dialogues as natural as possible, and the whole play was followed, day after day, by the interested audience, many of whom for the first time realized the solemnity and meaning of the stories they had often heard before. The first miracle plays given in England were acted probably soon after the Conquest. Among the earlier ones was the play of *St. Catharine*, which was performed in French about the year 1119. This custom of giving a play on a saint's day or other holy day was introduced from France by the Norman priests, and the play of *St. Catharine* was a favorite one with the English peasants, who learned, by the miracles represented, and the faithful picture of the martyrdom of St. Catharine as acted by the priests, a lesson of devotion and fidelity to principle, while being entertained by the unfamiliar method of instruction. This kind of entertainment at once proved so popular that the plays became a regular institution, and formed an important part of every special service, such as the consecration of a new church, the observance of holy days, the festivals of the saints, and so on.

The old monks who wrote these plays thought only of teaching their audiences religious truths, and used every means to deepen the impression they wished to make. Every detail that could interest was introduced, and the scenes on the stage were as faithful copies of the actual events as they could be made. If a play of the nativity were to be given at Christmas-tide, the audience saw before them, in a series of moving pictures, all the incidents of the beautiful Bible-story. There were the shepherds watching their flocks, silent and calm until they heard from the skies the thrilling greeting of the angelic hosts; then they could be followed to Bethlehem and seen kneeling beside the wonderful child, into whose presence came also the three Eastern kings, with royal gifts, to do homage. Nothing was omitted that would serve to illustrate the story, and no better means could have been found of teaching in an age when the mass of people were as ignorant as little children of the knowledge that could be had from books.

So in the play of *The Deluge* the audience saw enacted on the stage all the strange events mentioned in the story; and Noah and his sons, the ark and its furnishings, all became real to them, the story becoming even more vivid by the introduction of several incidents not mentioned in the Bible, such as the refusal of Noah's wife to enter the ark, the beating which she received from her husband in consequence, and other comic situations which the priests invented to give variety to the play.

The names of some of these old mysteries, such as *The Creation of the World*, *The Fall of Man*, *The Story of Cain and Abel*, are enough to show their character, and illustrate this new method of teaching.

The audiences became so large at last that

scaffoldings were built outside the windows for the accommodations of those who could not get inside the church ; but as the crowds who came to see the plays were continually trampling down the graves and defacing the church-yard, it was thought best finally to build the stage quite away from the church, and, though the actors were still the priests and choristers attached to the church, this was the first step toward infringing on the purely sacred character of the plays.

Later on the trade-guilds, or associations of drapers, goldsmiths, weavers, and other trades whose custom it was to parade the streets on festival days, carrying pictures and images of the saint whose day they were celebrating, were invited to join the priests in the processions which marched through the streets before the performance, and in which sometimes the whole play would be given in pantomime on a wheeled stage ; and this was another step toward putting the plays into the hands of the people.

In time the trade-guilds themselves gave the plays, each guild having a play of its own, which it performed on festival days. The actors were carefully trained and were paid for acting; the stage properties were as handsome as the guilds could afford, and the actors wore masks or had their faces painted to suit the characters they represented. These plays were generally given in sequence, one following another in due order. Thus the one guild would present the creation of the world, which would be followed by a play from another guild representing the death of Abel or the story of the Flood; and in this way the most important Bible-scenes were enacted in a series, taking from two to three days, and often longer. The spectators, who looked on from scaffoldings or windows, would see first the stage upon which was acted the creation, and this would pass on to some other street, while another stage came in sight on which would be acted the expulsion of Adam and Eve from Paradise; and so one pageant would follow another till the whole Bible-story was complete.

These old plays came in time to be known by the names of the towns in which they were originally given; each great town, such as London, Chester, Coventry, Dublin, was noted for a special set of plays, and, although most of them are now lost, enough are left to show us what they were like; the principal manuscripts are those of the Chester, Wakefield, and Coventry plays, amounting in all to about a hundred.

The mystery and miracle plays gave place in great degree at last to another kind of play in which, instead of angels, devils, and Bible-heroes, there were characters representing Goodness or Wickedness, and the object of these plays was not to teach the lives of the saints or Bible-history, but to convey some lesson by means of an allegory. These were known as *Morality Plays*, and the characters were called Patience, Hope, Pride, Anger, and so on, depending upon the nature of the play.

The moralities were generally written by the monks, and both those and the miracle plays show an interesting side of English literature between the twelfth and fifteenth centuries. They were very popular because they were so easily understood, and were a means of entertainmment and instruction in the days when few could read or write and nearly everyone depended for amusement upon the stories told by wandering harpers, or the tales of some returned palmer. During the festivals in which these plays were acted the entire population of the city gave itself up to amusement, the great crowds filling roofs, balconies, scaffoldings, and every available place for seeing, or following the long procession from one street to another in never-tiring wonder.

The religious character of the entertainment allowed the people to combine duty with pleasure, and a picture of one of the old English cities during the performance of one of the long plays would have shown people of all classes —monks, students, tradespeople, apprentices, mechanics, rich and poor, well-born and lowly— all bent on pleasure, and accounting the seeing of the play the only business in life.

The morality plays, though still acted with the miracle plays for long to come, were in turn followed by the *Interludes* and *Masques* which were so popular from the middle of the fifteenth to the middle of the sixteenth century, and which were a part of every entertainment given by state, or guild, or nobleman. The interlude was a satire or farce written in dialogue and spoken by persons who took on different characters. The masques were generally given in dumb show and dancing, no speaking being allowed.

These plays were not at all religious in character, though some of them resembled the morality plays. They were generally very short, and often were a play upon any question that was agitating the people, though as a rule they were merry and light pieces whose sole object was to amuse. The interludes and masques were very popular with the higher classes, and no entertainment was considered complete without them. They were constantly given at court and in the castles of the nobility, and lords and ladies of the highest rank often took part in them, though every nobleman had his band of trained actors who were ready at the shortest moment to perform.

In those days it was the custom for the higher nobility to give great entertainments lasting weeks at a time, to which the court was often invited, and at these times, which generally fell at Christmas, or Easter, or some other church festival, the interludes and masques were important parts of the amusement. They were usually given immediately after the feast, or before the last course had been served, and as no expense was spared in costumes and decorations the effect was often magnificent.

A picture of such an entertainment would be even more dazzling than a glimpse at one of the old morality plays, for the castle hall would be bright with beautifully dressed ladies whose silk and velvet robes, glittering with jewels and adorned with laces and feathers, would but rival the splendid costumes of the courtiers, with their jewelled swords, coats of bright-colored satin, and plumed hats. The stage was generally erected in the great hall, and the play was often acted by the lords and ladies. One of the old chroniclers records a masque which was given at one of the royal palaces during the reign of Henry VIII. in which the king himself took part.

A castle, with towers, gates, and battlements

was erected in the great hall, and garrisoned with beautiful ladies whose satin dresses were covered with leaves of gold, and who wore fancy head-dresses instead of helmets. This was Castle Dangerous, which had never yet surrendered to an enemy. But while the brave ladies were looking out of the castle windows and sighing for new adventures, there entered a company of goodly knights, of whom the king was one, wearing suits embroidered with gold and glittering with jewels, and they laid siege to the castle with great vehemence, for they had never yet been vanquished. And then, after a pretty scene of storming and resistance, the beautiful ladies surrendered and came out on the lawn and danced a graceful measure with the brave knights, after which they gave them possession of the castle, which immediately vanished as if by magic, and so the play ended without a word being spoken.

These plays, in which shepherds and shepherdesses, Cupids, Graces, and Muses took part, were very graceful and pleasing, and continued in favor for a great length of time.

When the interludes or masques were given in public they were generally performed in the pauses between the different parts of the morality plays, or during the great public feasts which were so numerous in those days, or at the universities. The performers in these plays, at first trained for the use of the nobleman in whose service they were, came gradually to extend their work outside the castle halls. They still wore the livery of their lord, and were under the protection of his name, but it came to be the custom gradually for these actors to go from one place to another and perform for the amusement of the people. Thus there grew up companies of actors, consisting of bands of players who were either in the employ of some lord or wandered from place to place giving their entertainments whenever they could get an audience, whether it were in the castle of some nobleman or in the town-hall, or in the inn at which they stopped.

The inns in those days were generally built around an open court-yard, and had galleries with windows opening on them running around each story. When a play was given the stage was erected in the court-yard, and the lower class of spectators stood on the ground while the more select witnessed the performance from the galleries.

But the acting of plays became so popular at last that special houses were set apart for the purpose, and in time theatres were built for the use and convenience of regular companies of players, though it still remained the custom for the monarch or any great nobleman to summon the company to play before him, as it would have been considered a degradation for any sovereign to visit a public theatre.

Hardly any attention was paid to scenery or stage properties in these old theatres. Sometimes a placard bearing the name of London, or Athens, alone denoting where the scene was laid, while a gilded chair beneath a canopy gave the idea of a palace, an altar stood for a church, and a table covered with bottles and tankards represented an inn. Generally the stage was strewn with rushes, and sometimes, during the performance of heavy tragedy, the whole stage was hung with black to add greater solemnity to the scene.

The earliest playwrights after the monks were the actors themselves, whose practical knowledge of their art did much to make their pieces successful. But dramatic literature for a long time was of such a poor character that it hardly deserved to be placed among the works of writers of other classes; for although, from the time of the first miracle plays, early in the twelfth century, down to the ages of Chaucer and Caxton, plays were written continually in England, there was hardly one produced which showed more than mediocre talent, with the exception of those which were taken directly from the Scriptures.

Among the old writers of plays John Bale, who lived about the middle of the sixteenth century, may be mentioned as a playwright who did not limit himself to the masques and interludes which were then so much in fashion, but who looked into the old chronicles of England and found there stories more interesting than any that could be imagined. From this source Bale drew the materials for his historical play of *King John*, which showed an English audience how interesting the history of their own country could be when put on the stage, and this play, with one or two others by other writers, founded the historic drama which later English dramatists carried to such heights.

Another play acted about the same time was founded on the story of Palamon and Arcite, already familiar through the work of Chaucer. The author of this play was Richard Edwards, who was appointed by Queen Elizabeth master of the choir-boys in the Royal Chapel, and who was also known as a writer of many good poems and interludes. Perhaps the most popular writer of interludes was John Heywood, who wrote many of these plays while a resident at court, where most of them were performed. But though the interludes and masques were so much liked they were but the introduction to the real drama, which first appeared in England in 1561 with the first English tragedy. This play was written by Thomas Norton and Thomas Sackville, and was given at the Christ-

22

mas festivities in Westminster. It was called *The Tragedy of Gorboduc*, and was taken from Geoffrey of Monmouth's *History of Britain*.

Gorboduc, King of Britain, desired to leave his kingdom to his two sons Porrex and Ferrex; but on asking advice from his council, one advised him to let the eldest son Ferrex have the whole, another advised him to follow out his first wish, and a third to keep the kingdom himself and divide it equally by will. But Gorboduc took his own way, and immediately fell into trouble, for Ferrex was jealous of his brother and Porrex feared for his life. Both rushed to arms and the news was carried to Gorboduc, who, before he had time to interfere, was shocked by the appearance of a messenger bringing the news of the death of Ferrex by his brother's hand. Porrex was summoned before his father, who reproached him for his brother's death, and Porrex asked for no mercy, but said that the whole trouble came from the division of the kingdom. He remained at court, but before his father passed sentence upon him he was slain in his sleep by his mother, who was distracted by the death of Ferrex. Then the people rose and slew both Gorboduc and his wife, after which there was civil war until a king was chosen by common consent.

This play, though differing entirely from the masques and interludes in the treatment and conception of the plot, had yet something in common with them. Every act was preceded by a masque in which the progress of the play was given in dumb show. Thus, immediately before the act in which Gorboduc receives tidings of the death of Ferrex, a band of mourners, clad in black, enter and pass three times around the stage; and before the act in which the queen slays Porrex there is a masque in which the Furies drive before them a king and queen who had murdered their children, and so on.

As the English of that day were familiar with the horrors of civil war and the discords which shook the kingdom during the disputes about the succession, this first English tragedy could be well understood by them, as representing a scene from their national life, and this, together with its origin in the old British chronicles, made it distinctly an English play. It was performed by the gentlemen of the Inner Temple, where the Christmas festivities were held that year.

The first English comedy was written by Nicholas Udall, head-master of Eton. It was called *Ralph Roister Doister*, and was written for the Eton boys, who were in the habit of giving some Latin play at Christmas. *Ralph Roister Doister*, which was written in English, was a lively satire against vain boasting, and was characteristic of the English race in its ridicule of bluster and self-praise, thus making both the tragedy and comedy English from the beginning.

Ralph Roister Doister was a blundering swaggerer who paid court to Dame Custance, a fair widow who was already betrothed to a merchant who was away at sea. Custance received the attentions of Ralph just for the fun of seeing him made ridiculous, and the plot is based on this. The play is very bright and merry, and the fun is entirely free from the coarseness which is found in so many of the old comedies and which was so characteristic of the times.

Among the early English dramatists who be-gan to write at the time when the drama proper began to be distinguished from the interludes and masques was a group of men who are gen-erally classed together, because their work on the whole partook of the same general charac-teristics, and was marked by about the same degree of merit.

These men were in nearly every case gradu-ates of a university, and had the education which it was thought necessary for gentlemen of birth and breeding to possess.

Among these may be mentioned Lyly, Greene, Nash, Lodge, Peele, and Kyd, who are known sometimes as the "university wits," to distinguish them from a number of playwrights who had no advantages of birth or education, but yet whose experience as actors enabled them to write plays that were very acceptable to the public, because the authors were ac-quainted with the practical details of the stage and had that command of dramatic effect which is so necessary in making a good play.

But the "university wits" were also often actors, many of them going on the stage as soon as they left the university, and the practical knowledge of their art, combined with a liberal education, enabled them to produce those plays which first gave distinction to the English drama and placed it in the realm of pure literature.

Among the plays written by these authors are the *Endymion* and *Sappho* of Lyly, modelled after the classic writers and founded on the Greek myths; the *David and Bethsabe* of Peele, who was remarkable for the beauty of his language, power of description, and pathos; the *History of Friar Bacon* by Greene, *The Spanish Tragedy* by Kyd, and *The True Tragedies of Marius and Sylla* by Lodge.

Although none of these plays are great, yet they are of sufficient merit to place their authors among the founders of English dramatic literature.

Most of this group died young, after leading

very profligate lives, but their work had certain qualities which will always make it interesting to the student of literature.

But the English drama was surely if slowly rising toward the great perfection which it reached in this century, and the year 1563 saw the birth of an author whose works placed the drama at once on a higher level than it had yet reached. This was Christopher Marlowe, the first writer of plays whose genius at all compared with Chaucer, the greatest poet up to the sixteenth century, nearly of the same age with Spenser and Sidney, and endowed with a mind of such rare qualities that the brilliance of his fame is yet undimmed.

Marlowe was educated at Cambridge, and is included in the group of university wits. Immediately on leaving college he joined a company of actors, his ready wit and careless good humor winning him a cordial welcome among those who had apparently given up all serious aims in life and who lived only for the hour. Marlowe was the wildest among this set of wild companions, who were utterly regardless of authority and stopped at nothing that promised amusement or change.

But while he was thus giving himself up to idle and foolish pastimes, he was at the same time laying the foundations of the English drama on lines so strong and bold that his works will always be regarded as among the best in English dramatic literature.

Marlowe's first play, *Tamburlaine the Great*, the story of a Scythian chief whose conquests sound like a fairy-tale, did not show the greatness of his genius, though it won him immediate fame ; this was due, however, to the character of the hero, who was just such a boaster and ranter as the public at that time delighted in, for coarse humor and unrefined wit were both highly appreciated by the old theatre-goers.

But *Tamburlaine*, if it did nothing else, at least made Marlowe's name familiar to the public, and predisposed it in the author's favor, and this was much, at a time when the playwright could only count on popular favor for his daily bread.

The History of Dr. Faustus, founded on the

old German legend of a philosopher who bargained his soul away for a certain number of years of earthly power and enjoyment; *The Jew of Malta*, a play which depended for its interest upon the character of a Jew as he appeared to Englishmen in the fifteenth century, when to be of Jewish blood made one liable to be considered as a monster, or only half-human; and *The Tragedy of Edward II.*, showed Marlowe at his best, and the force and inspiration of these works at once placed the author among the greatest of English writers. He can be compared only to the great dramatists who succeeded him, for preceding playwrights do not approach him in the power and greatness of his genius. He died at the age of thirty, but even in his short life accomplished more than any dramatist up to his time and made himself a name not unworthy of being placed near that of Shakespeare.

Children's Stories in American Literature

By HENRIETTA CHRISTIAN WRIGHT

12mo, $1.25

This new volume will add another great success to those which the author has already achieved in writing instructive books for children in the three fields of literature, science, and history. Nothing could be more welcome at this time than a book which brings our own literature within the realm of the Grammar School where the study should rightfully begin. Miss Wright has made it easy for the child to become interested in reading by making the personalities of the writers stand out in a most striking way. Eliot, the translator of the Bible into the Indian language, Irving, Cooper, Bryant, Prescott, Hawthorne, Bancroft, Longfellow, Whittier, Mrs. Stowe, Lowell, and Parkman are considered and treated with constant reference to that side of their works and personalities which most nearly appeals to children.

"Miss Henrietta Christian Wright has a most delightful style and tells just what everyone desires to know about his favorite author. She knows how to seize upon the salient points of an author and use these to the best advantage. The use of such a book in the schools will inspire students with a love of American literature and the best reading."

—Teachers' World.

"Personally, the writer has felt the need of just such a book since his first year of teaching. The stereotyped histories of literature are too abstract and cold. The children can't get close to the characters. While to-day we want to study the real literature, yet teachers are constantly searching for the lives of our writers; books that not only contain information, but books that will be read by all children. This book contains the best collection of stories and authors I have ever seen. It is neither stiff, formal nor weak. They are, in my opinion, the best biographies I ever read that were prepared for school use—either for high school or college, and, at the same time, are written in such a way as to hold the attention of the ten-year-old or the college professor who has learned to see the man behind the writer. Truly a new day is dawning for writing a book for children, and this book is one of the best I have seen."—*North-Western Journal of Education.*

"These 'Children's Stories of American Literature' are full of interest and information calculated to benefit young readers in many ways. They are not what the title of the book would seem to indicate—childish stories written in childish language, but sketches of the lives and writings of our great American authors, written in elegant style and diction."

—Journal of Education.

Children's Stories in American History

By HENRIETTA CHRISTIAN WRIGHT

With 12 full-page illustrations, from drawings by J. STEEPLE DAVIS

12mo, $1.25

CHILDREN'S STORIES OF AMERICAN PROGRESS

By HENRIETTA CHRISTIAN WRIGHT

With 12 full-page illustrations, from drawings by J. STEEPLE DAVIS

12mo, $1.25

"To the teacher or parent the Children's Stories will prove a boon. Sketches so clearly and charmingly told as these will surely rivet the attention of a little reader even when there is a book of fairy tales to follow."
—MRS. BURTON HARRISON.

The former of these volumes deals with the remote and partially legendary episodes of our earlier history, while the latter contains pictures of events of the first half of the present century, and comprehends all the prominent steps by which we have reached our present position, both as regards extent of country and industrial prosperity.

Miss Wright displays a remarkable talent for vivid and picturesque narration, and a child fond of story-telling will gain from these books an amount of information which may far exceed that which is usually acquired from the rigid instruction of the schoolroom. The simplicity of the author's language and her easy and natural method of treating the interesting events of our national history especially fit the volumes for school use. They have already been adopted for this purpose in a number of prominent cities throughout the country, including New York and Brooklyn, and in every case they have given the utmost satisfaction.

Children's Stories of the Great Scientists

By HENRIETTA CHRISTIAN WRIGHT

With numerous full-page portraits.   12mo, $1.25

Equal in interest and value to Miss Wright's two previous books which have attained such popularity as supplementary readers. It deals, in a simple, entertaining manner, with sixteen of the great men of science, giving a brief, readable account of their lives and of what discoveries they made.

CONTENTS

I. Galileo and the Wonders of the Telescope, 1564–1642—II. Kepler and the Pathways of the Planets, 1571–1635—III. Newton and the Finding of the World Secret, 1642–1727—IV. Franklin and the Identity of Lightning and Electricity, 1706–1790—V. Charles Linnaeus and the Story of the Flowers, 1707–1778—VI. Herschel and the Story of the Stars, 1738–1822—VII. Rumford and the Relations of Motion and Heat, 1753–1814—VIII. Cuvier and the Animals of the Past, 1769–1832—IX. Humboldt and Nature in the New World, 1769–1859—X. Davy and Nature's Magicians, 1778–1829—XI. Faraday and the Production of Electricity by Magnetism, 1791–1867—XII. Charles Lyell and the Story of the Rocks, 1797–1875—XIII. Agassiz and the Story of the Animal Kingdom, 1807–1874—XIV. Tyndall and Diamagnetism and Radiant Heat, 1825—XV. Kirchoff and the Story Told by Sunbeam and Starbeam, 1824–1887—XVI. Darwin and Huxley.

CHILDREN'S STORIES IN ENGLISH LITERATURE

TALIESIN TO SHAKSPERE   SHAKSPERE TO TENNYSON

By HENRIETTA CHRISTIAN WRIGHT

2 vols., 12mo, $1.25 each

" Miss Wright sets forth in simple attractive language the lives and works of the great men in English literature. Miss Wright has endeared herself to a host of young readers by her stories of progress, history, and science, but she has never before produced a book so thoroughly fascinating as this."—*Boston Beacon.*

PRESS NOTICES.

"The author selects prominent events and of these gives a concise yet graphic account. Her fresh and animated style imparts a new interest to these oft-told stories, and insures the absorbed attention of old as well as young."—*The Critic.*

"Miss Wright is favorably known by her volume of well-told 'Stories in American History,' and her 'Stories of American Progress' is equally worthy of commendation. Taken together they present a series of pictures of great graphic interest. The illustrations are excellent."
—*The Nation.*

"They are told in a singularly free and colloquial way, and each chapter is made more valuable by being opened with a swift and graphic glance over the antecedent time and events which led up to the particular points described. The illustrations add to the book's other points of attraction for young readers."—*Chicago Times.*

"Told in a style to entertain and instruct. The work will be appreciated by all who desire to cultivate early in their children a taste for disciplinary, as well as useful reading. It has good illustrations and is handsomely bound."—*Boston Globe.*

"A beautiful as well as a valuable book for young readers is 'Children's Stories of American Progress.' The book will be of service to juvenile readers in interesting them in historical studies."
—*Boston Transcript.*

"A most delightful and instructive collection of historical events, told in a simple and pleasant manner. Almost every occurrence in the gradual development of our country is woven into an attractive story for young people."—*San Francisco Evening Post.*

*** *Correspondence is solicited in regard to copies for examination and terms of introduction.*

CHARLES SCRIBNER'S SONS, Publishers,
153–157 Fifth Avenue, New York.

www.ingramcontent.com/pod-product-compliance
Lightning Source LLC
Chambersburg PA
CBHW021747110726
47902CB00006B/1434